BELOVED ENEMY

Margaret Carr

CHIVERS

| British Library Cataloguing in Publication Data available |

This Large Print edition published by BBC Audiobooks Ltd, Bath, 2008.
Published by arrangement with the author.

U.K. Hardcover ISBN 978 1 408 41273 2
U.K. Softcover ISBN 978 1 408 41274 9

Printed and bound in Great Britain by
Antony Rowe, Chippenham, Wiltshire

CHAPTER ONE

'Who the devil is it?' Roger Fenleigh thundered at his bewildered accountant and friend of many years' standing.

'I'm afraid I don't know. I didn't realise there was a sitting tenant on the estate,' came the reply.

'You say there is no evidence of any rent payments?' the taller and darker of the two men snapped as he paced backward and forward in front of Simon Osbourne's desk.

'None at all.'

'So where has this person come from two weeks before I sign a contract of sale?'

Simon Osbourne, of Osbourne, Osbourne and Clark, rose from his chair and walked around the desk.

'I was talking to a chap last week from the Tyne Tees Television lot. He was babbling on about some up-and-coming writer. He said she lived on Greensfield Estate. I told him it must be a mistake, as nobody had lived there since your great uncle. He was most insistent, so when I came back to the office I went through every file I could find and nothing. Next day I sent young Phillips out to the estate and he came back with the news that a person was living in the old boathouse.'

'Squatter!' Roger spat out.

'More than likely,' his friend agreed, settling himself on the edge of the desk top. 'Move them on in no time, you'll see.'

Roger Fenleigh stopped his pacing and, turning a cynical smile upon his friend's beaming confidence, said, 'The letter of the law, eh, Simon?'

'Quite, quite so.'

'No go, I'm afraid. I'm going down there now and if I find any trespassers, heaven help them.'

'Look here, Roger, that won't help anything.'

Simon thrust himself away from the desk and hurried after his friend who was striding purposefully towards the door.

'Isn't it a bit late in the day? I mean, why don't we go down together on Monday?'

'Goodbye, Simon, have a good weekend and give the family my regards.'

Roger Fenleigh left the building that housed Osbourne, Osbourne and Clark and crossed the road to a pedestrian passage that led him back to the multi-storey carpark where he had left his car. The red sporty model glowed in the drab light between the concrete pillars of the half-empty carpark. But for once the sight of it did nothing to lift the scowl from its owner's face as he lowered himself into the driving seat.

The car shot down the ramp and out on to the street with a squeal of tyres. Once through the city and out on to the open road, the frown across his brow disappeared and the tightness around his shoulders eased. Driving always helped him to relax and clear his mind for the next move. It was this ability to click problems through his brain, like slides through a projector, that had helped him get so far and do so well.

In the twenty years he'd been on his own, he had worked his way up through building sites and part-time education to university, partnerships, directorships and eventually to the expensive consultancy he now enjoyed with the mammoth building conglomerates. Work was his pleasure from waking to sleeping, driving him along as did the purring engine beneath the bonnet of the car.

With a click he set his present problem under his mind's eye and thirty minutes later turned off the main road on to a narrow, country lane. A short distance farther on he swung the car in through two tall stone pillars, alongside one of which dangled a dilapidated gate resting against a confusion of trees and rhododendrons. The house, when it came into view, was of mellow stone in the classic lines of its Georgian architecture. Everywhere, weeds, ivy and moss encroached, blocking out light from sleeping windows, pushing up through gravel and stonework.

The house meant nothing to him. Oh, he admired it for what it had been, a beautiful house in its heyday, but he had never lived there, nor even visited. He'd never heard of great Uncle Chesterton and had been as surprised as anyone when notified of his inheritance. Now, on only his second visit, his eyes wandered knowledgeably over the front of the house. It was a plain rectangle of solid construction with rows of tall sash windows. The entrance was enclosed by tall columns and covered in by a hood. The roof fell backward from each side and the front slope was pierced by a row of dormer windows. His fingers plucked the bundle of large keys from the pocket of his driving coat as he approached the main entrance.

It was early March and the light was already fading. Simon had been right to advise him to wait. Of course it would have been far better to inspect the place in daylight, but he was here now and might as well take a look around. Pale statues stood sentinel in alcoves around a square, marble-floored hall. Deep doorways gave on to large, shuttered rooms, until he came to a library. Bookshelves lined three walls of the room, their shelves still stacked with books. He ran his fingers appreciatively along the bindings.

Leather skirts hung down from the shelves above to protect the books beneath from dust. Grilled doors at floor level guarded tomes of ancient script. Heavy drapes were tied back from the windows and the evening light

4

showed no dust sheets on a large, central table or a high wing-backed chair to one side of the Adam fireplace. Someone still used the library, he noted, running a finger across the dust-free surface of the table.

Heading up the main staircase to the second floor, he moved from room to room and window to window. There was still enough light to survey the surrounding parkland in front of the house. He traced the river's course along what he knew to be the western boundary, until it disappeared into the uneven edge of the wood.

'That's where it will be,' he told himself, calculating distance and direction.

Leaving the room with every intention of finding his way to the boathouse, he was distracted, when passing an open door on the right at the head of the stairs, by a flash of something bright on the hillside behind the house. He crossed the space to stand looking out of the window. It was the bright red of an anorak worn by a girl silhouetted against the darkening sky. Her hair and skirt flew out around her in wild disarray as she stood on the outcrop as though carved from the same stone.

Minutes passed as he watched, then without warning she was gone. As though released from a dream, he turned to leave.

A sharp crack was the only warning before he was hurled forward across the floor, gathering splinters in his hands as he tried to save himself. It was seconds before he recovered his wind and attempted to sit up. When he did, the cause of his accident became painfully obvious. He had gone through the floor, or at least one of his feet had. When he twisted to try and release the trapped ankle there was an ominous grinding sound and the pain increased to a point where black clouds threatened his consciousness. After much grunting and groaning, he managed to break away the surrounding rotten floor boards and ease his foot from the trapped shoe. Gritting his teeth, he made his way to the head of the stairs.

*　　　*　　　*

Penny Chapman stood on a rocky outcrop overlooking Greensfield Park. Tuck, the retriever, lay panting close by while the two other dogs, Bonnie and Clyde, foraged for rabbits. Bonnie was half collie and had to be watched when in the vicinity of sheep but Clyde was only fifteen weeks old and as yet his lineage wasn't showing.

Penny's skirt whirled around her legs as the winter sun slid from the one and only patch of blue sky. A jet screamed overhead, a blade of grey steel, slicing into the encroaching evening. The wind, that was a constant factor here on the high moors of North Northumberland, gently coiled Penny's long hair around her throat only to snatch it back again and whip it across her eyes. A tumble of stones down the hillside behind her heralded the return of Bonnie and Clyde.

'Come on dogs, time for home,' she said.

A soft mist cloaked the river that ran like a stocking from the estate below her to the grey line of the sea on the horizon. The dogs ran ahead as she climbed down on to the narrow sheep track that would lead them back to the broken wall that had once surrounded the park, but was now only a pile of scattered stones.

They scrambled over the wall and crossed the wilderness of parkland that had originally been set out by the famous Capability Brown. Turning the corner of the kitchen garden, Penny was startled to see a red sports car standing in the drive. She looked around the wide sweep of weed-covered gravel and back to the tall house whose surroundings failed to dim its elegant beauty.

Where was the owner of the car? Surely they couldn't be in the house. There was no electricity on and it would soon be dark. She looked for signs of a torch light flickering in any of the windows, but there was nothing, no movement anywhere. Puzzled, she walked over to the heavy door which gave at her touch. The dogs were in like a shot, scrambling around in the darkening interior. Penny was familiar with the house and moved from room to room easily in the shadowy light. The furniture, shrouded in dust sheets, made eerie shapes in the grey background but it held no fear for her, only loving memories.

'Hello, any one here?' she called.

The ground floor revealed nothing. As she made her way back into the hall, a muffled sound from above brought her to the foot of the sweeping staircase.

'Hello, anyone there?' she repeated.

'Upstairs, on the left!'

The voice, strong, male and full of angry frustration made her jump, even though she was half expecting it. Cautiously, she made her way up the stairs and found the open door of one of the main bedrooms. Inside the room was dark and she could only just make out the shape of a large man sitting on the far side of a four-poster bed.

'Thank goodness,' a deep voice growled.

'Who are you?' she asked, her voice spiked with suspicion.

'Well, I'm not a burglar if that's what you're thinking and I'm in no fit state to attack anyone, so for heaven's sake come in where I can see you.' She was standing in the doorway surrounded by curious dogs.

'I didn't think you were a burglar, not with a red sports car. But why are you in no fit state to attack anyone even considering they would let you?'

He still hadn't risen from the bed.

'Because I think I may have broken my ankle.'

Penny moved into the twilight that drifted through the window. The dogs, taking this as a sign of approval, came into the room, sniffing enthusiastically.

'Look, keep those dogs away, will you? The last thing I need is for one of them to bump me.'

She called to them and they came and lay down quietly beside her with the exception of Clyde, who disappeared beneath the bed. The stranger gave a sharp sigh and spoke in a different tone of voice.

'I don't know who you are or where you are from or what you're doing here on this estate but do you drive?'

The question took her by surprise.

'Er, no,' she answered.

'Drat! Do you live nearby?'

'Yes, but I don't have a phone. If you can't walk then I shall have to go to the village and call for an ambulance from there.'

She felt rather than saw the keenness of his gaze from the heavily-shadowed corner where he sat.

'I know a little first aid,' she offered. 'Perhaps I could help.'

'Thank you, but I'm not in the mood for amateurs.'

A slither of moonlight touched the window and fell across Penny's face as she turned

9

away. An awkward silence hung in the air.

'How far away is this village?' he asked wearily.

'Two miles from the end of the drive but I'll take a short cut through the woods and be back as quick as I can.'

'Woods, at this time of night? Will you be safe?'

'Quite safe.'

'Right,' he said, nodding in agreement.

She left the house and crossed the park to her home. She was there before she realised Clyde wasn't with her. She'd been so angry at the stranger's rudeness that she had failed to notice the puppy's disappearance. She had already resolved to ring the emergency services from the village then return straight home without going back to the house. Now she would have to go back, if only to collect Clyde.

A good hour had passed before Penny returned.

'Where the devil have you been?' the man demanded. 'I thought something had happened to you.'

'My home was on the way so I stopped to leave the dogs and collect these.'

She held up a large torch and in its light, a flask. It was completely dark now and she stood the torch on the tallboy to give them as much light as possible, before carrying the flask to the bed. Here, she could see for the

10

first time the man she was helping. His face was sharp and angular in the shadowy light, silhouetting the strength of well-shaped bones. His lids drooped over his eyes at the sudden intrusion of light from the torch but the tightness of his mouth betrayed his awareness of Penny's scrutiny.

Long fingers raked self-consciously through ruffled fairish hair. The once immaculate blue suit was crumpled and smudged with dust.

'You missed that one,' he said and pointed at the small bundle fast asleep in the centre of the bed.

'Yes, he's the reason I came back,' she said pointedly.

The remark hit home and the scowl left his face.

'I owe you an apology,' he said, as he took the cup of hot tea from her hands.

She inclined her head as she sat down with care on the end of the bed. With the smaller cup of tea in her hand she was placing the flask on the floor.

'How did you hurt your ankle?'

There was a short pause before he said, 'My own stupidity entirely. I allowed myself to be distracted by a view from one of the top floor windows.'

Penny nodded her head.

'The views are wonderful, aren't they?'

'You know the house?' The tone of his voice didn't change but he was immediately alert.

11

Penny watched the swirl of tea in her cup and remembered how Becker, the old housekeeper, had made up marvellous futures for her from the tea leaves. She sensed his impatience.

'Um, I knew the late owner. Was it the floor?'

He turned to look at her.

'Yes, I went through the floorboards. Once through I couldn't get the wretched foot out again. I think I did most of the damage at that point. The place is in a dreadful state. It wasn't until I tried to get back down the stairs that I realised how bad the ankle was. I managed to get on to this bed then I must have passed out. When I came to the light was fading and I had visions of rotting up here.'

'Doesn't anyone know you are here?'

'Only one person and he was going off for the weekend, so you see it would have been quite some time before anyone found me. I'm very grateful you were around, but tell me, how do you come to be here?'

'I was out walking with my dogs when I saw your car in the drive. I knew there was no electricity on in the house, so I put two and two together and thought I had better look into it.'

'Lucky for me that you did.'

He gave her the shadow of a smile and rubbed a hand across the beginnings of roughness on his chin.

12

'You must know the area well. You knew there was no power in the house. You talked of taking a short cut to the village, so I assume you must be fairly familiar with the place.'

'Yes, I suppose you could say I was.'

'So you would know if there was anyone living on the estate.'

'The owner of the Hall died two years ago and lived abroad four years before that.'

'Oh, I don't mean here in the Hall. There have been rumours of a squatter living somewhere on the estate, in a boathouse, I believe. Do you know anything about that, maybe seen a stranger around recently?'

'A squatter?'

'Yes.'

'No.'

Something went cold inside her as she watched him trying to ease his ankle. The straight mouth was pulled back in a grimace. A lock of hair fell over his forehead, he looked up, quickly catching her glance in his own.

'How do you know this person is a squatter? Perhaps they are perfectly legitimate and own the property,' she enquired.

'They don't.'

'You sound very sure.'

'I am. You see, I own the estate.'

Penny felt every muscle in her body tighten with shock.

'You own the estate!'

'Yes. You seem surprised.'

She had the full force of his attention now.

'I don't mean to be rude,' she said, when she had recovered sufficiently from his announcement, 'but as I explained before, I knew the last owner and I hadn't heard that the place had been sold.'

She was shaking right down to her toes.

'Are you perhaps questioning my right as legitimate owner, Miss—er?'

There was a hint of amusement in his voice.

'Chapman,' Penny muttered automatically. 'Penelope Chapman. I'm just puzzled, that's all.'

'Well, to satisfy your curiosity, Miss Penelope Chapman, I inherited the Hall from my late great uncle, Charles Algernon Chesterton, whom I never met, nor even heard of until contacted by a solicitor. You, I take it, knew the gentleman personally?'

Penny closed her eyes against the pain and nodded.

'Could I have another cup of tea, do you think?' he asked.

'I shouldn't. You may need an anaesthetic when they set your ankle. It could make you sick.'

Her hands trembled as she fastened the cups back on to the flask.

'Are you planning to live at the Hall? It will take an awful lot of renovation work,' she inquired.

'No. I live in town. I only came up here

14

today because of these rumours.'

'You have no immediate plans for your inheritance then?' Penny asked hopefully.

'Yes, I have plans. I'm in the middle of selling the place and they won't take kindly to finding they have a sitting tenant. That's why I must find this person, if they exist, and quickly.'

'You're selling?'

'As long as I can deliver on time, yes.'

'Why is time so important?'

'Because these are busy people and they have strict schedules to keep.'

He rubbed the top of his leg, unconsciously trying to soothe the pain below it.

'What will these people do with the land?'

He gave her a long look before replying, 'They'll clear it and build houses. That's what's needed in this area, isn't it?'

'Clear it!'

Penny's foot sent the flask rolling across the floor to crack against the skirting boards. Clyde woke up with a start, saw his owner and bounded across the bed.

'I must let him out,' she said, grabbing the puppy and making her way out of the room as fast as she could, ignoring the grunt of pain that had come from the man as she'd leaped from the bed.

By the time the puppy had wandered around and done his business, the ambulance had arrived. In the ensuing activity, there was no more time for conversation. The house was locked up, the ambulance doors slammed and the tail lights disappeared down the drive.

CHAPTER TWO

The following Tuesday, Penny was on a bus into Newcastle. Mr Laing, of Roberts Laing and Hope, had been her husband's solicitors from his coming of age. Old Laing had died before Penny's time and young Reggie Laing, as her husband always referred to him, had taken over his affairs. She would tell him her story and hopefully that would put an end to the stranger's plans. Surely, as Charlie Chesterton's wife, she must be the rightful owner of the estate. Perhaps this was what Charlie had foreseen when he insisted that they should marry.

She had slept little over the past weekend, running the images of her encounter with the supposed new owner of Greensfield Hall through her mind again and again, trying to remember every word that had been said. Would she be too late in making her claim, she wondered, now that this man thought he owned the estate. The window of the bus threw back the image of her face as she watched the passing scenery. What would she do if she was? Where would she go?

She was relieved to relate her worries to the solicitor.

'If what you tell me is true,' he said when she'd finished 'and if as you say you can verify your marriage with documentation, then, yes, your marriage revokes any previous will.'

Reggie Laing, to Penny's surprise, had turned out to be an elderly man with a long, narrow face whose gold-rimmed spectacles sat precariously upon his nose. He was polite if somewhat distant at being asked to fit this urgent appointment into his busy schedule. As she told her story, she could see that her news shocked him. He looked along his bony nose as she remained silent.

'I must say, you have been an extremely naïve young woman. Did you really think you could come back to England and carry on as before without notifying anyone? Your husband was a careless man where legal matters were concerned, Mrs Chesterton. His will was made many years ago, long before you went to stay with him. The estate might have been sold and the monies gone to charities. Did you not think to enquire?'

Penny stared at the desk but her eyes were seeing Charlie's expression of deep concern for her future security.

'I'm sorry. I realise I have been foolish in delaying matters so long but I have already explained how difficult it was for me at the time of Charlie's death.'

'Quite so,' the solicitor said, rubbing his nose with a forefinger.

'I'm sure my husband knew of no other relative. I never heard him mention one.'

Her eyes dropped to her hands lying quietly in her lap. She had learned at an early age the futility of expressing anger or frustration. Emotions were not allowed at the orphanage in which she'd grown up. You stuck up for yourself or you kept yourself aloof. You never showed fear or eagerness.

Mr Laing spread his hands and sighed.

'A search was made for relatives, his will simply stating that in the event that no family member was forthcoming on his death then everything was to be sold and the money dispersed to his favourite charities. Mr Fenleigh recognised his grandfather's name as brother of the deceased and made contact with us bringing with him proof that he was indeed Mr Chesterton's great nephew. In all probability, Mr Chesterton did not know of his relative's existence, since Mr Fenleigh admitted to having no prior knowledge of his great uncle. Seemingly, the family parted company many years before in bad blood and neither side had made any effort to keep in touch with the other.'

There was a long silence while the solicitor tapped on the desk with the end of his pencil.

'We will, of course, write to Mr Fenleigh acquainting him with the new situation. But this is all very unfortunate and many adjustments will have to be made on both sides.'

Penny rose to her feet and shook the hand

being extended to her across the desk.

'You will be hearing from us again in due course, Mrs Chesterton.'

Though probably meant to be encouraging, it sounded more like a threat to Penny as she left the office.

*   *   *

'Well,' Roger demanded, 'are you going to tell me what you found out or are you going to continue to stuff yourself in that disgusting fashion?'

'Sorry, but you did invite me to dinner.'

'All right, now what did you find out? Who is she and how soon can you get rid of her?'

Simon swallowed the last piece of lemon meringue pie and looked thoughtfully at his friend.

'You did find her, I hope,' Roger queried impatiently.

'Oh, yes, I know of her.'

Roger's eyes narrowed.

'Know of her?' he said quietly, sitting perfectly still, his gaze never flinching.

'The lady is Charlie Chesterton's wife. She went to see Reggie Laing on Tuesday morning.'

Apart from a small twitch in his friend's jaw, there was no sign of the bombshell that had just exploded between them.

'Is that possible?' Roger asked.

'Undoubtedly. She has her marriage certificate. Reggie will be verifying it with the Portuguese authorities, of course.'

'Portuguese authorities?'

'They were married abroad. Mrs Chesterton failed to contact the solicitors on her return and that is what has caused all the confusion.'

There was a long, drawn-out hiss of escaping breath as Roger sat back.

Simon rose from the table and started to walk towards the door.

'Where are you going?' Roger demanded.

'I thought I would leave you to it, long day and all that.'

'Not likely. Hand me that cushion and help yourself to a drink. Make mine a double. This ankle is giving me gyp.'

'How long will it be in plaster?'

'Six weeks, so they tell me, if I haven't bashed it off before then. So it's old Charlie's widow who is living in the boathouse.'

'Yes.'

'There was no money to speak of so how does she intend to look after the place, I wonder.'

'Presumably by living in the boathouse and letting the rest take care of itself.'

'That deal with Trenchard's is worth a lot of money. Perhaps we can come to some arrangement with the old dear,' Roger decided.

A smile crept along Simon's mouth.

21

'I don't think so. You see, there is something I haven't mentioned yet.'

'Enlighten me,' Roger snapped.

'Mrs Chesterton isn't an old dear, but a young woman in her twenties.'

Roger snapped to attention.

'So, we have a little gold digger instead,' he said with a curl of his lip. 'He must have been old enough to be her grandfather twice over.'

'Seventy-nine, to be precise.'

'Well, this makes it easier. We'll buy her off. Her sort always has a price and with the money Trenchard is offering we can afford to be generous.'

Simon looked sceptical but said nothing. The conversation turned to Roger's lady friend.

'This will put paid to the Easter holiday,' he said, rapping the ankle with his stick.

'Have you told her yet?'

'You know Elvera, she's never in one place long enough to tell her anything.'

'You're like ships that pass in the night. Don't you ever want to tie her down?'

'I can't see her married somehow, can you?'

Elvera Minhurst was a tall, beautiful redhead with her own production company. She travelled the world's trouble spots with a small film crew. A total professional, she scorned the more domesticated of women.

'Is she going to move in with you?'

'No, we suit very well but I value my

22

freedom too much to share my home with anyone.'

Simon cast a quick glance around one of the largest of the luxury riverside apartments. Elegantly furnished, there were two bedrooms, en suites, a study, a cloakroom, as well as the long living area with its raised dining platform and french windows leading out on to the balcony which overlooked the river. Elvera had a studio flat in town but Roger worked from home when he wasn't travelling around various building sites.

'Have you ever taken a holiday, Roger?'

'Never had the time.'

'You should ease up, you know. It's not as if you have to work so hard any more. Why don't you come home with me this weekend? My parents would love to see you. It's not as if you can do much with that thing on your ankle and only a daily to take care of you.'

A heavy scowl pleated Roger's brow as he considered his friend's invitation. It would be warm and welcoming, he knew, and the only snag would be Fran, Simon's divorced sister. For some reason, the Osbournes were convinced that she would make him a good wife. Nothing was said outright, but the suggestion was there hanging over him like a cloud.

The light of hope that always lit up Fran's face when he arrived was most uncomfortable. He was never at ease with women who wanted to fuss over him. His preference was the independent type, like Elvera. The Osbourne family home was like a very rich cake—something you took a bit out of occasionally but never indulged in!

'Right, Simon, I'll enjoy that, thank you,' he conceded finally.

Several days later, Penny opened the door of the boathouse to find a man of medium height, smartly dressed, with blue eyes and dark hair, standing on her threshold. His hand was raised as though about to knock.

'Mrs Chesterton?' he asked, once recovered from the shock of having his move anticipated.

Two lines appeared between her brows for she had never used her married name and didn't understand how he knew it.

'Yes.'

'My name is Simon Osbourne. I'm Mr Fenleigh's accountant and he has asked me to come to see you on his behalf due to an accident that has left him rather incapacitated.'

'Mr Fenleigh? Oh, yes,' she said, her brow clearing as she remembered the name the solicitor had given her for the man with the broken ankle. 'Then you had better come in.'

'I'm sorry about the mess,' he excused himself while brushing loose leaves and twigs from his jacket and shaking the muddy bottoms of his trousers one after the other. 'That's a dreadful path you have.'

He spoke over the noise of the barking dogs.

'You've obviously come through the woods. If you'd driven up the main drive, it's just a short walk across the lawns.'

Simon gave a low smile.

'I asked in the village and was told the quickest way was through the woods.'

'Well, strictly speaking, I suppose they were right, but quickest isn't always easiest.'

Penny led them across the room to a deep-seated settee where he sat down with a grateful sigh and spread his damp feet across the gold and brown hooky mat before the wood burning stove.

'Can I get you something hot to drink, Mr Osbourne?'

'Thank you, that would be very nice,' he replied.

When Penny opened the door into the kitchen, the dogs flung themselves past her, bent on satisfying their curiosity. The puppy dashed up to Simon, wagging his tail, certain of an equally enthusiastic response. Bonnie sidled up alongside the settee and gave him a quick once over. The retriever ambled forward, sniffed thoroughly around the damp ankles and lay down. Simon sat stiffly, overwhelmed by all the attention until Penny returned.

'I don't understand, Mrs Chesterton, why you have never brought this marriage to light before,' he said, accepting the cup of tea she offered and dipping hungrily into the barrel of biscuits.

'Is Mr Fenleigh going to contest my claim to the estate?' Penny asked.

'He's been advised not to. As the wife of the late owner, your position is the stronger, even if a little late in the day.'

Penny placed the biscuit barrel and her mug of tea on the small table and turned her favourite rocking chair around to face her visitor.

'I knew nothing of legal procedures, Mr Osbourne. All I was aware of was that this had been our home for some years. Mr Chesterton was anxious that it should continue to be my home after he died. To that end, he asked me to marry him.'

'But surely he meant you to sell the property and live off the proceeds. How else could you afford to look after such a large property?'

Penny slowly shook her head.

'He knew I loved it here, knew I would never sell it.'

Felling uncomfortable, Simon remarked, 'Mr Fenleigh was led to believe that there was no money with the estate, so unless you have a private income how do you intend to maintain such a large place?'

'That's my business, Mr Osbourne, but since presumably you have been sent here to find out information for Mr Fenleigh, then I shall tell you that I earn enough to support myself here in the boathouse. As for the rest of the estate, I haven't really thought about it. Perhaps I could sell the house and the grazing when my ownership is established.'

'I doubt if anyone would be interested in the house without the land. Why do you want to keep all the land? Why not keep a small, manageable amount for yourself and sell the rest with the house?'

Penny took a deep breath.

'So that some big contractor can tear it all down and build houses?'

Simon's eyebrows shot up in surprise. She could tell he was wondering how she had acquired the information.

'I know all about Mr Fenleigh's plans and I am not trying to be difficult for the sake of it, truly, but I cannot allow such destruction of a beautiful place. If I could sell the house and land to someone who would restore it and care for it as a personal home, then I would. But I'll never have it turned into a housing estate.'

'There are few people who could afford to turn a place of this size into a single home,' he reminded her. 'And it could become a tremendous financial burden to you whether you live in it or not.'

He smiled as a cold nose snuffled his hand until a gentle mouth took the biscuit that had been dangling forgotten in his fingers.

27

'I'll find a way somehow,' she said anxiously.

'Will you not consider letting Fenleigh go ahead with the deal and take a share of the profits which could be substantial?'

'No.'

'Very well,' he said, rising to his feet. 'I am sorry, but I had to try. It goes with the job, I'm afraid.'

His smile was lopsided, apologetic, and Penny decided he really was a nice man.

'That's all right, I understand. You can tell Mr Fenleigh I will never sell him the park. I will do all in my power to keep it as it is. I am sorry that my lack of experience and know-how has caused him a disappointment over the will. Please give him my apologies.'

Alone once more, Penny pulled on her anorak and called the dogs. She needed some air and activity. She turned towards the village and her one real friend, Claire Sutcliffe. Claire owned an antique cum curio shop which she ran with the help of her son and grandfather. Her marriage had broken up five years previously and she had bought the shop and the flat above in the village high street in an effort to keep together what was left of her family.

Claire was in her forties, plump with dark curly hair and hazel eyes. She was motherly and a good listener and bought Penny's sketches of the characters in her children's books. They sold well once Billy, Claire's son, had framed them. It was after Penny's initial timid approach to Claire about her sketches that their friendship blossomed.

Now, they sat together in the back room of the shop. Bill was out with the van collecting a chest of drawers and Arthur, Claire's grandfather, was busy in the large shed at the back of the building that served as a workshop, where he restored old furniture. Claire listened patiently as Penny told her of the accountant's visit.

'It's not as though,' Claire said when Penny at last fell silent, 'you want to keep the estate entirely for your own benefit, is it? I mean the local people walk in the woods. Kids play there, men fish there. It's in everyone's interest that you continue to keep the place as it is. True, new houses would be welcome in the village but they aren't going to be the kind of houses that youngsters around here can afford. It'll be one of those commuter estates with well-off strangers who will either not want to be part of the village life, or they will be stepping in and trying to take over within weeks. It will change everything around here and not for the better, I'll bet.'

Penny waited.

'Well,' Claire prompted, 'don't you see what I'm getting at?'

The dogs lay all around their feet and Clyde looked up and woofed as a tall young man with brown curly hair came in shaking rain from his shoulders.

'You must give the estate to one of these Trusts,' Claire continued, 'like the National or English Heritage, or some such. They will restore the house and take care of the grounds for you. You could have it written into the contract that you keep the boathouse and whatever land you want. Simple.'

Penny was surprised that she hadn't thought of that herself.

'But doesn't it have to have some historical significance or be of conservation interest?'

Claire shrugged.

'So what? We'll research it for you. If you dig deep enough, you can always come up with something to take their interest. Billy and Grandad will help, won't you, Billy?'

Billy nodded. Penny was smiling now.

'I remember Charlie telling me that the Chesterton who had ordered the building of Greensfield had been a friend of the Prince Regent.'

'Well, there you are then,' Claire said triumphantly.

Penny's confidence was swelling as she took her leave.

'I'm so glad I came. You've given me something to aim for because if a Trust can be persuaded to take over the estate then nobody is ever going to be able to build on the land.'

During the next few days, Penny received a letter from Osbourne, Osbourne and Clark requesting she attend a meeting with Roger Fenleigh. When she arrived in the offices, there was no-one else in the waiting area. After waiting patiently for twenty minutes, she was convinced they had forgotten her. No-one else had arrived which meant that either it had been cancelled and she had not been informed, or they were already in there. The receptionist jumped as Penny appeared before her desk.

'I think I have been overlooked,' Penny said.

'No, not at all,' the girl answered glancing nervously at a door somewhere down the corridor. 'They'll buzz me when you're to go in.'

At that moment, there was a burst of loud, angry voices issuing from the door the receptionist had indicated.

'Is that Mr Osbourne's office?' Penny asked.

' 'Fraid so,' she said with a shrug.

'Who's with him?'

'A client.'

'Mr Fenleigh?'

'That's right.'

A dreadful feeling grew inside her, turning her face bright red. She glanced back at the receptionist who had once more replaced her earphones and was typing away. Penny rose to her feet and moved down the corridor to stand outside the door through which the angry voices could still be heard. She recognised the smooth voice of Simon Osbourne immediately.

31

'For heaven's sake, Roger, it's a bit thick to call her a tramp and being unreasonable isn't going to get us very far, is it?'

Then Roger Fenleigh's fierce tones!

'No, but her motives in marrying a man of seventy-nine are certainly dubious, are they not? If you are trying to tell me these are not the actions of a gold-digging strumpet then I wouldn't give you tuppence for your opinion because nobody is going to believe this woman married a man old enough to be her grandfather for love alone.'

Penny staggered back from the door as though she had been shot.

'Tell them I couldn't wait,' she told the startled receptionist as she ran through the waiting area and out of the building.

Tears of pain and rage convulsed her as she hid in a narrow alleyway alongside the building. After a while she was able to regain some control and made for a quiet café on the opposite side of the road. Here she ordered tea and sat gazing blindly through the grimy window.

Time lost importance. She had heard nothing she secretly knew everyone would feel when they knew of her circumstances, which was why she had been reluctant to reveal her marriage in the first place. Fenleigh had only put those feelings into words, yet hearing them spoken with such venom and disgust had nearly broken her heart.

A face she recognised was staring at her through the window. A second later, a voice interrupted her thoughts.

'Fancy meeting you here. May I join you? Sally, the receptionist, said you had left in a hurry.'

Simon Osbourne pulled up a chair and sat down without waiting for her permission.

'He really hates me, doesn't he?' she said vaguely.

Simon's mouth twisted.

'Ah, I thought it must have been something like that. You overheard us?'

'It was difficult not to.'

'Can I get you another cup of tea?'

'No, thank you.' She attempted to pull herself together. 'I must get back to the bus station.'

'No need, I'll drive you home.'

Penny started to protest but Simon would have none of it.

'No, I insist. It's the least I can do.'

So she gave in and allowed herself to be led back to the rear of his office and helped into his car. They drove in silence for most of the way. Then Simon spoke without taking his eyes off the road.

'You loved Chesterton very much, didn't you?'

'Yes.'

'I don't understand why he didn't think to protect you earlier with a new will if he thought so much of you.'

Penny smiled.

'Practicalities never concerned him. He rejected any thoughts of dying until near the end then he did what he considered was the next best thing.'

'Roger is a hard man,' Simon said after a pause. 'I'd be the first to acknowledge that but I have never known him be anything but fair in his business dealings. What you overheard were words spoken in the heat of the moment. I've known him a long time and he . . .'

'Please, he's your friend, I understand,' Penny said matter-of-factly.

CHAPTER THREE

Over the following weeks, she heard nothing at all. Then on returning from her morning walk through the fine drizzle of yet another wet day, she saw a man sheltering beneath the eaves of the boathouse. Her first reaction upon seeing him there was that perhaps it was someone from one of the Trusts she'd contacted come to see the property. They met at the bottom of the steps, the dogs fussing around their feet.

'Mrs Chesterton, I presume?'

She tipped back her head pulling her yellow so'wester off as she did so.

'What can I do for you, Mr Fenleigh?'

'Good heavens, it's you!' he exclaimed, a look of horrified disbelief on his face. 'You married my great uncle?'

The tone of his voice made Penny cringe, but she kept her cool.

'I don't know why you're here. I thought I had made my feeling on the subject of the estate perfectly clear to your Mr Osbourne.'

'He tells me you're prepared to sell the estate to a private owner. Is that correct?'

'I don't see how that concerns you.'

A small nerve jerked along his jaw bone as icy eyes stared at her.

'I know of someone who may be interested.'

Penny dropped her eyes to the ground and

chewed on her lower lip. If this someone was a friend of his, what was to stop him selling the property back to Fenleigh, who would then presumably dispose of it as he had intended all along?

'No, Mr Fenleigh, I don't think so,' she said shaking her head.

'You have so many buyers knocking on your door you can afford to be choosy?'

'That's not the point.'

'Then what is?'

'I'm hoping to find a buyer who will never allow building on the estate.'

'And how do you propose to pin down any prospective buyer to that agreement, supposing you can find one, that is?' he asked, raising his eyebrows in irritation.

The wind blew rain into where they stood but Penny refused to be hasty or intimidated. With an angry hiss of breath he turned to look out across the lawns to the main drive where his waiting car stood.

'Coming down here has cost me time and effort I can ill afford,' he snapped.

Penny glanced down at his now healed ankle.

'Then I'm surprised that you came.'

'The least you can do is offer to show my friend around the property. You can't possibly know whether they will agree to your ridiculous terms or not until they are allowed to see it for themselves.'

36

He had pulled up the collar of his coat and was peering out in the direction of the Hall.

'I really don't see the . . . ' Penny began, only to be cut off by his persistence.

'Shall we say the day after tomorrow, two-thirty?'

'Well, if you must.' Penny sighed.

'Good.'

He headed out into the rain leaving a subdued Penny amidst a swirl of impatient dogs chivvying her towards the steps. Drat the man, she thought, angry at herself as well as him. It was the first time she had seen him in full daylight and he was just as impressive as she had suspected the night she rescued him. His appearance here today had sent her heart into overdrive and she couldn't for the life of her think rationally now he'd gone.

Two days later, the sun shone, making up for the preceding wet weather. Penny took the dogs for a long walk before heading down to the village to catch the two-hourly bus into the city. A poster in the village bakers had caught her eye the previous day. It was advertising an environmental talk to be held in the city library that afternoon. There were to be a variety of speakers but one in particular stood out for her. It was a Mr George Hazell of the Richmond Trust, the signatory of the most hopeful reply she'd had regarding the possible future of the estate.

As soon as she had seen the poster she was

determined to attend the lecture. Please, she thought, please let them agree to take over the Hall. She couldn't bear to think of the consequences if she had to sell to someone like Roger Fenleigh. What would happen to the deer who came down to the river to drink in the evening when the trees on the far bank were black lace against the sunset, or the swans who nested on the same little island every year? Would they cut down the trees belonging to the squirrels, move on the owls and bats who flew up and down the water and clear out the small inhabitants of the river banks? She shivered at the thought and rubbed her hands in agitation.

She had a quick sandwich in the small café attached to the library building before going into the lecture. The large room was three quarters full. Four speakers sat at the top table. Penny took a seat on the edge of an aisle with a clear view of the speakers' table. A tall young woman with floppy blonde hair and purple framed glasses came forward to introduce the speakers. When it came to George Hazell's turn, there was a short film show. He showed some of the work the Trust had done in restoring historic buildings and areas of land under threat. Penny decided that she must speak to him after the talk was over, if the opportunity presented itself.

When the lecture was over and each speaker had been heard, drinks were handed

38

round and Penny found her chance to speak to George Hazell.

'Ah, Greensfield Park, wasn't it?' he said.

'That's right. I don't want to be a nuisance but I just wondered if you might know how the Trust regarded my application.'

'They give every application fair consideration,' he said and smiled reassuringly.

'If they decide to go ahead what happens next?'

'They send you loads of questionnaires to fill in. Nothing to worry about. Three avenues they cover, personal, historical and financial.'

'Financial?' Penny squeaked, the frown on her brow deepening.

George Hazell tried to smooth the way.

'There has to be some kind of endowment to cover the cost of running the place.'

'But I don't have any money, that's why I thought of the Trust.'

'Don't worry. If the estate is interesting enough, there are other ways of raising the money. Charities, the lottery, it all depends what our historian comes up with.'

Penny left in a thoughtful mood and knew, without glancing at her watch, that she had missed the four-thirty bus and would now have a two-hour wait. She was standing by the kerb waiting to cross the road to the bus station when a car pulled up alongside her.

'Where the devil have you been?' an angry voice bellowed at her.

Penny jumped and took a second look. Roger Fenleigh and a beautiful redhead had drawn up in a four-wheel-drive. He climbed out of the car, ignoring the line of traffic behind him, and grasped Penny's arm.

'I thought we had arranged to meet at two o'clock so you could show my friend around the property. We have been all the way out there for nothing and here you are waltzing around town.'

Still talking, he propelled her into the back seat of the car without as much as a by-your-leave. Suddenly a car from behind pulled out and squeezed through between them and the on-coming traffic. Then a motorist parked at the kerb wanted to get out and started honking his horn.

'You're holding up the traffic,' Penny cried as he bundled her in and slammed the door.

He climbed back into the driving seat totally unconcerned at the chaos around him and started moving forward into the traffic.

'Where are we going?' Penny demanded.

'Back to the Hall. How else are we going to get to see the dratted house?'

'Look, I'm terribly sorry about missing our appointment. There was this lecture I wanted to attend and I completely forgot about you wanting to see the property. Anyway, I really don't see that there is much sense in you trekking all the way out to Greensfield again today. If you just put me off at the next bus stop I'll make my own way home.'

The woman beside him hadn't said a word.

'Late afternoon is not a good time to look around the Hall as you know,' Penny continued.

'Ah, but this time we will have someone with us to keep us out of harm's way.'

Penny fell silent, exhausted by her efforts to dissuade him.

'This is Ms Minhurst, by the way, your prospective buyer. Elvera, my great aunt Chesterton.'

Penny made a great effort to stifle the sick feeling that rose up from her stomach.

'Penny Chapman,' she said, leaning forward to offer her hand to the woman in the front seat.

Penny felt dowdy in her red skirt and jumper with a black jacket, shoes and old leather shoulder bag. Her large blue eyes met Elvera's brown-eyed stare in the driver's mirror momentarily and she felt herself blush.

What was this smart woman, in her lavender silk designer suit and wool jacket with her beautiful hair in a smooth chignon, to Roger Fenleigh? Was it as she had supposed a put-up job to allow the estate to be used for development? Was she his live-in partner? Simon Osbourne had said he didn't believe in marriage.

Thirty minutes later they arrived in front of the house.

'Shall we go in?' he asked when they came to a halt.

They stepped from the car and crossed to the great oak door where Roger produced a heavy bunch of keys.

They stepped on to the marble floor of the hallway and Penny felt like a traitor about to betray her best friend.

'Shall we start where the evil deed was done?' he said.

Lost to his reasoning, Penny hesitated.

'The attic bedrooms,' he said as though trying to make himself understood to a rather slow child. 'The accident—my ankle—your heroic rescue.'

Penny turned away.

'It's a beautiful house,' she said almost to herself.

'It's neglected,' he growled.

'Oh, but it wasn't always like this.' Penny's voice warmed despite herself as she led the way upstairs. 'It had a staff of fifteen at the turn of the century. There's a small staircase goes up from the kitchen to the staff rooms above. The attic rooms belonged to the children.'

They were on the second-floor landing now.

'There's a nursery and schoolroom, nanny's room and the governess's room. Can't you just imagine it, so full of noise and activity?'

'Not really, no,' Elvera Minhurst said. 'I thought children were seen and not heard in those days.'

'For heaven's sake, come out of there.'

Roger grasped Penny's arm pulling her back and up against him as she had been about to enter one of the rooms.

'We don't know how many patches of rotten flooring there are.'

'It's safe this end. I know because I come up quite often.'

She pulled away from him, breathing a little heavier than she would have expected.

'Yes, well, perhaps coming up here wasn't such a good idea after all.'

'The house isn't really in all that bad a way for its age,' Penny said, turning to the woman still standing at the top of the stairs.

Now why am I sounding so eager when I don't really want her to have it? Penny scowled at the contradiction in her thoughts.

'How many rooms are there on this floor?' Elvera asked.

'Six, four at the front and two at the back, with two large walk-in linen cupboards.'

'Shall we go down?' Roger suggested, as though having lost all interest.

Penny preceded him down the staircase to the first floor.

'The main suite has bedroom, bathroom and dressing-room. There is a similar suite in the west wing directly opposite where we are now and three further bedrooms, oh, and a small room above the front entrance, which used to be the sewing-room.'

'Where is the guest bathroom?' Elvera asked, twisting around to count the rooms.

'There isn't one. Charlie lived alone for most of his life and a large part of that time he was travelling.'

They moved on through the east wing suite, bedroom and dressing-room before coming to a halt in the entrance to the bathroom. Penny scuffed her toes in embarrassment as the air whistled through Roger's teeth.

'The old man used this?'

This was a bathroom suite of gigantic proportions, heavily panelled in carved mahogany. The bath was hooded to at least two feet above Roger's head and topped with an ornate canopy. The hand basin, in a marble surround, had brass towel rails on either side and a mirrored back stood against the far wall dressed in floral china dishes. The toilet was something else again and Penny had to bite down hard to stop herself from laughing at the look of incredulity on the couple's faces. It rose majestically from three wooden steps around its base to long mahogany shoulders that supported the bowl. On the wall behind, great columns spiralled upward like the pipes of a cathedral organ!

'He didn't actually use this one.' Penny smoothed her features. 'This was mine.'

She watched Roger struggle to find a suitable expression. Their eyes met and held,

44

first with a challenge that slowly melted into smiles and then they were doubled up with laughter.

'I'm glad nobody pulled the plug on you,' he said, then let out another great peal of laughter.

Elvera stared at them with raised eyebrows then turning back to the room was heard to mutter, 'I must get the film crew up here.'

'What do you do for a living?' Roger asked Penny as they descended the stairs.

'I write for children and as a great concession from the publisher I am allowed to illustrate my own books. I also illustrate woodland animals and a friend sells them for me when they have been framed.'

'You must be quite talented,' Roger said in a surprised tone of voice. 'Simon said the television people told him about you originally. Why would that be? Are you some famous person I should know?'

'Not at all but I read some of my stories on a children's programme.'

'That's more than most of us could do.'

Penny regarded him warily, not trusting this new side of his character. 'Three hundred thousand for the lot and you can keep the boathouse,' Elvera said suddenly.

Penny stared at her for several seconds, completely stunned.

'What did you say?'

Elvera repeated her offer, and Penny

glanced up at Roger Fenleigh who was standing so close she could taste his breath on her lips and feel the icy shards from his eyes pierce her own.

'No,' she said.

'So what would you accept?' Elvera asked over her shoulder as a slim hand with painted nails reached out and stroked Roger's arm in a proprietary way.

'It isn't a question of price. It's whether or not you will agree to protect the estate.'

'In what way?'

She had swung round and was observing Penny from narrowed, brown eyes which oddly had no depth or softness. Penny took a deep breath.

'There will be a contract forbidding you to sell the land for development.'

'I see. Well, it's a bit early to be talking about selling, isn't it, when all I am looking for is a home?'

She shrugged the padded shoulders that supported her outfit like a clothes hanger over her exceedingly slim figure.

'Why don't you put an offer in writing, dear, and see if Mrs Chesterton can refuse it?'

Roger Fenleigh tucked the woman's arm through his and escorted her to the car as he spoke. Penny watched them leave. Had she been wrong to turn down the offer, she wondered. She was certain now that it was all a put-up job, but supposing the Trust wasn't interested. A mass of doubt and indecision chased around in her head.

But it wasn't really the deviousness of the offer that hurt, it wasn't even the sale of the property at all. It was the sense of humour she and Roger Fenleigh had shared, if only for a moment, the joined laughter in the bathroom, that had felt so natural yet had been so false that it really hurt.

CHAPTER FOUR

Elvera Minhurst's offer arrived in the post two days later. She had raised the price by twenty-five thousand pounds. In the same post came a card asking her to confirm a date for a visit from a Mr Cooper of the Richmond Trust. She wrote back agreeing to a date in twelve days' time.

Later that afternoon, she was sitting at the table in the library of the old house where she often went to work when she heard a noise behind her. She half turned to find Roger Fenleigh watching her from the doorway.

'I thought I would find you here. I called at the boathouse but all I got was a chorus from the dogs.'

Penny opened her mouth to object to his intrusion but was forestalled when he raised his hands.

'The door was open.'

He lowered himself into the dustsheet free chair by the fireplace without waiting for permission and reluctantly she turned back to her work.

'I want to know if you are going to sell to my friend.'

'Why?'

'Because I'm still not convinced you won't sell to me in the end.'

'You mean the people who were going to build houses here have decided to wait after all?'

'No, we've lost that deal but there are other opportunities equally lucrative.'

'Don't you want your friend to have the house?'

'Not if it means tying her down to that silly contract of yours.'

Penny couldn't withhold the smile that flitted momentarily across her lips. 'So you were going to buy it from her and sell it to the developers.'

She was incredibly pleased that she had successfully squashed his plan.

'What would you have done if I had already been in residence at the Hall when you returned from Portugal? Thrown me out?' he inquired.

'No, of course not,' she said quite assuredly.

'Then what?'

When she didn't answer he made an impatient movement that broke her thoughts.

'I don't know.'

'Let's get this straight. If I'd been living at the Hall and there had been no mention of selling the estate you would have come to me and offered to split the estate and continued to hide your marriage. I could have retained my family home and several acres and you would have kept your boathouse and the woods. Is that how you see it? A nice, cosy arrangement, no fights no squabbles.'

Penny moved uncomfortably on her seat for wasn't that exactly how she had seen it?

'But you weren't in the Hall, Mr Fenleigh, and I will guard this estate from developers if it kills me.'

'How? You can't afford to keep it and you won't sell it because no-one with an ounce of sense is going to buy a property with your conditions attached to it.'

His scorn needled her to say, 'I may already have found the answer to that. The Richmond Trust has shown an interest in the estate.'

He sat back in the chair.

'I see, and what do you think will happen to your precious estate if that happens? Visitors will want toilets, a restaurant, shop and walkways. You can bet the river won't escape either. Its banks will be cleared of dipping boughs and sheltering reeds and replaced by shorn grass. Picnic areas will abound and play areas for children. And there goes your tranquillity.'

He leaned forward now, arms slung across his open knees.

'What gives you the right to keep me from my inheritance? A piece of paper that says you took advantage of a senile old man? No?'

His quick turnabout from acceptable stranger to tormentor was too much for Penny. The shock froze her features and turned her insides to liquid as he went on.

50

'Why did you marry my great uncle? You're young, beautiful, talented. Why would you want to hide yourself away in some forsaken spot with only an old man for company?'

'The country was beautiful and your great uncle was always wonderful company.'

'What was the old fool thinking of to leave such a helpless waif in a situation like this? He must have been off his head.'

'If you lived to be a hundred, you would never grow above the height of his knees,' she blazed at him. 'I loved him,' she declared and to her shame tears sprang into her eyes. 'If you've quite finished, please leave.'

'What kind of love could you share with a man of his age?' he goaded.

Pushing back her chair too quickly, her foot clipped the chair leg, throwing her over the seat. With nothing for her outstretched hands to reach for and the feel of the chair tilting beneath her, she braced herself for the thump, only to have two hands pluck her to safety at the last minute.

It took her a minute or two to realise that she was being held close to him and for only a second it felt like where she wanted to be. Then he was gently setting her aside and righting the chair.

*   *   *

Roger Fenleigh watched the change of

expression on Elvera's face as she read through Penelope Chapman's letter. She was a very sensual woman. Her titian hair glowed in the light from the gas fire. Her wide shoulders gave the sense of power to the sleek body which tapered down to strong legs. A jungle cat in human form, she thought, in more ways than one. It was a jungle instinct that came to her aid when tracking down what he thought of as her victims, coming home with taped interviews and film footage unavailable to media rivals.

They had known one another for three years, most of that time spent apart. The initial attraction had worn thin, he realised with a start, and they had become a habit, their lives sliding side by side along the same track.

'So your plan didn't work.'

She laid down the letter and moved over to a drinks cabinet.

'I didn't really expect it to. I've lost Trenchard's so I think I'll just call it a day.'

Elvera came back, handed him a glass of whisky and curled up in a chair opposite him.

'But it's your home by right of family inheritance! You can't just give up on it surely.'

Roger gave a heavy sigh and stared down into his glass.

'It would seem I have no alternative.'

'That's a pity.'

'Oh, I'm sure she will be only too pleased to let you film her outrageous bathroom.'

'I wasn't thinking about myself. I was thinking of you. I've been thinking just lately you look in need of a rest. It would be handy to have somewhere like Greensfield Park to go to when you could spare the time.'

His brows met as he frowned.

'Alternatively, I could give up the apartment and live there permanently. There is room for several studies, the size of the one I have here, on the ground floor alone. With more room for extended technology I wouldn't need to travel as much. But she isn't going to sell.'

'She will, for the right price. She'll have to eventually.'

Roger polished off his drink then replied, 'Not to us.'

'She has someone else interested?' Elvera asked.

He gave a harsh laugh.

'A trust, the Richmond Trust. She is under the impression that they will take it over for her.'

'And will they?'

'Not without a large endowment.'

'Which she doesn't have. So all we have to do is wait.'

'She's a fighter, Elvera, and there are all sorts of charities and the lottery to which they could appeal. A lot depends on their initial research into the house itself.'

He ran a hand through his hair in a weary gesture.

'I'll take a quick shower then we'll get off.'

He didn't feel in the party mood but he'd promised Elvera they would go to a club where she was hoping a certain celebrity would show. Once put into words, the thought of possessing Greensfield Park rested very comfortably in his mind. Images of open log fires, long walks with a dog and a smell of home cooking to come back to stirred forbidden clouds of how a real home might feel.

He stepped out of the shower and shook the water from his eyes, then after a brisk dry and a quick shave he dressed in evening clothes.

In the meantime, Penny had received word that the representative of the Richmond Trust would call, as promised in her earlier correspondence.

Mr Cooper was a tall, thin man in his thirties with stooped shoulders and heavy rimmed glasses. Penny gave him what information she had gleaned from Charlie over the years, about the house and family.

'I believe the family line ends with a certain Mr Roger Fenleigh, your union not having been blessed with children,' he said discreetly.

He towered over her as she turned to correct him.

'He may be the last of the Chestertons, Mr Cooper, but I am the owner of Greensfield Park.'

He looked rather startled.

'Yes, quite. I didn't mean to suggest

otherwise. Hopefully Mr Fenleigh will marry and carry on the family line. It's so sad when these old families die out. Of course the family is much older than the house, you understand.'

He began a lengthy and detailed account of the Chesterton family history that stretched back to 1066 and the Battle of Hastings. The dialogue lasted from the boathouse steps, across the lawns and over the drive to the house entrance where it lasted a further forty-five minutes! Penny then left him to his survey.

It was growing dusk when he knocked once more on the boathouse door. The excitement glowed in his eyes as he burst past her into the room.

'You are an extremely fortunate young woman, Mrs Chesterton. I have found diaries dating back to the seventeenth century. You have a unique library, the contents of which have seemingly never been exposed to external scrutiny.'

Penny screwed up her eyes in an attempt to understand the historian's excited babbling. Then her mind cleared.

'Oh, do you mean Charlie's grandmother's diaries?'

'They were the last of the Chesterton diaries. The first one was written in 1651, just two years after the beheading of Charles the First.'

'I assumed they were all grandmother Anne's.'

'No, not at all. There have been several authors, the first of whom was a Charlotte Anne Chesterton who went into exile with her father after the Battle of Worcester.'

'Will these diaries be enough to raise the interest needed for the Trust to take over Greensfield Park?'

'Not in themselves, no. It will need verifying of course, but if it is genuine, it will rewrite the history books.'

Penny was becoming impatient.

'What will, Mr Cooper?'

'The marriage of one Charles Stuart to Mary Cavendish as witnessed by Charlotte Anne Chesterton.'

'What? Charles the Second was married while still in exile?'

Penny felt suddenly faint.

'Of course, you realise this must be kept strictly between ourselves. I will inform the Trustees of my discovery and you should be hearing from them shortly.'

After he'd gone, Penny sat down in her rocking chair and wondered what can of worms she had opened now.

A week passed with no word from the Trust, then a second week and Penny began to wonder if the astounding discovery was to be swept under the carpet. Penny had now made it her business to read through the diaries. Apart from the one entry referring to the marriage, there was no more mention of Mary

Cavendish and Penny couldn't help but wonder what had happened to her.

Penny walked down to the village later that week with her latest batch of illustrations for Claire. There were customers in the shop when she arrived and an agitated Claire directed her into the back shop. Penny's gaze wandered idly around the tiny back room until it fell on a pile of children's books lying in a plush buttoned chair opposite. As she bent forward to pick one up, a newspaper which had been jammed down the side between the books and the arm of the chair, slipped on to the floor and fell open. A short article halfway down the page caught her attention.

A local novelist's claim to diaries that purport to show that Charles the Second of England was already married to the daughter of an English cavalier before later marrying the Portuguese Princess Catherine of Braganza is disputed. A family member is prepared to go to court to prove the diaries belong to him and disclaims all knowledge of how the Richmond Trust's historian was made aware of what is considered private family documents. The Trust, unaware of this dispute, has since withdrawn its interest in the family property of Greensfield Park.

Claire heard Penny's gasp of shock as she came in from the shop.

'I was hoping to warn you before you read it.'

Penny had picked up the paper and was reading it again.

'What are they talking about? I haven't made any claims. I am the real owner. It says the Trust is withdrawing their interest. Why? I don't understand any of this,' she cried, turning to Claire. 'How could anyone have known about the diaries? Mr Cooper was most insistent that no-one should be told.'

'I take it they haven't been in touch with you since.'

Penny shook her head.

'It's him, isn't it, Roger Fenleigh? He's done this to force me to sell to him. Who else could it be?'

'I don't know. Who else have you told?' Claire's voice was full of sympathy.

'No-one, not even you.'

'I'll make us a cup of tea.'

'Did someone mention tea?' Arthur said, appearing from the bottom of the stairs. 'Remember the couple that came round to see the house the other week? The woman was in my workshop yesterday. Told me Brian Reed from the pub told her where she could see some real furniture what might suit the house.'

'Which house?' Penny asked.

'Greensfield Park. That was what you were

talking about, wasn't it?'

'You see,' Penny said to Claire, 'it was him. They're already convinced it's theirs.'

The old man had taken his tea and wandered out again.

'Drink your tea, Penny, and try one of these biscuits. I made them last night from a recipe of my grandmother's but the men didn't take to them. I want your opinion.'

Penny bit into the biscuit.

'It's very nice.'

'Is that all? Very nice condemns it! I won't be making any more.'

Penny laughed.

'Oh, come on, they aren't that bad.'

'Well, it was worth it just to see you laugh again.'

Back at the boathouse, Penny took the key down from the back of the kitchen door, bid the dogs stay and left to cross to the Hall. Once there, she left the main door open. It was a sunny day, and dust motes danced in the sunbeams through the dirty windows as she entered the library, her favourite room. She sat down in the winged chair by the empty grate and wondered what Charlie would have made of her present predicament. She hadn't been there long when she heard the sound of a car arrive, the car door slam, then came the squeak of rubber soles across the marble floor of the hall.

'I know you are hiding in that chair.'

Penny rose from the chair, her expression calm, her hands pushed down in her pockets. With a snort of disgust, Roger Fenleigh pushed himself away from the doorway and came towards her.

'Why do you always make me feel like the wolf to your Red Riding Hood?'

Penny made a great effort to lift her chin and outstare him.

'You had the Trust back off, didn't you? And now you want me to sell to you and we are back to square one.'

'I don't know what you are talking about but if the Trust has backed off then it's for the best. I have come here today to make you another offer. The deal I had with the builders has fallen through and I don't need to look for another buyer now but I am interested in your vision of how it might have been.'

'Excuse me?'

A wiry smile twisted his lips and deepened the line down his cheeks.

'Oh, I think you remember. You in your boathouse and me in the Hall, no fights, no squabbles.'

'It wasn't a vision, Mr Fenleigh, merely a solution had you already been ensconced in the Hall. But you weren't.'

'No, and you haven't a buyer so I'm offering four hundred thousand for the house and parkland. You can keep the boathouse and the woods and any free rights of way you want.'

'No, Mr Fenleigh.'

'For heaven's sake, drop the Mr Fenleigh bit. My name is Roger.'

'No, Mr Fenleigh, I will not sell you the house, not now, not ever and that is my last word on the subject.'

She put out a hand to feel for the chair and sat down with a thump as she heard the door slam behind him.

CHAPTER FIVE

In town, to buy correction tapes and ribbon cassettes for her typewriter, a few days later, Penny was pushing her way along the crowded pavement towards the kerb, with the intention of crossing the road. When she made to step into the road, someone called her name. As she looked over her shoulder, she was blind to the car that was heading towards her.

Faces swam all around her, blotting out the sky, mouths opening and closing, like fish starved of air. Noise roared in her head then drifted off to a whisper, to return once again in waves. A coat was placed over her, a young man argued with an elderly lady, then green arms reached for her. She knew there was something she should say, as she answered questions, but all she felt was fear.

Faces appeared and disappeared. Strange sounds and smells rubbed at her senses. A curtain swished to one side and a nurse came up to the bed.

'Hello, can you tell me who you are?'

An ache throbbed behind her eyes and her hand rose to rub at her temple.

'Penelope Chapman.'

'Good and what day is it?'

'Thursday. What happened?'

'You're in Casualty at the General,' the

nurse replied, a wide smile appearing. 'You were knocked down by a car in Grainger Street but not to worry, there's no bones broken. A few cuts and bruises, mind, but nothing life threatening. How do you feel?'

'Horrible. My head aches.'

'You have a slight concussion so we want to keep you in overnight. Is there anyone you would like to contact?'

'Only a friend, to ask if she will look in on my dogs.'

She must have gone to sleep after that for the next thing she knew was the feeling of movement and the sound of rubber wheels squeaking on polished floors as she was wheeled to a ward. She awoke with a start next morning as a trolley trundled past. She was on the point of climbing out of bed when the nurse arrived, a bottle of tablets in her hand.

'I had these made up at the dispensary for you. They are pain killers and will save you having to travel to a chemist if you live out in the country. Take two when you get home and another two every four hours. They will cover you for the weekend then if you are still feeling under the weather go to your own doctor. You can get up and get dressed if you feel well enough but you mustn't leave until the doctor has seen you.'

On her own again, Penny slid her legs over the edge of the bed and stood up, clenching her eyes tight as pain shot through her head.

She was stiff all over with a knee that didn't seem to be working properly and a bandage on her right arm made getting into her clothes difficult. At last she was ready and she sat down with a sigh in a chair next to the bed.

She was startled when the nurse arrived at the foot of her bed with a policeman in tow.

'The officer would like to talk to you before you leave.'

She gave Penny a quizzical look before bustling off again. The policeman wanted to know if she had felt anyone push her into the road. Penny smiled hesitantly.

'No.'

'A witness says they saw someone push you as they brushed past you in the crowd. You don't remember feeling pushed just before you fell?'

'I don't remember anything about the accident, I'm afraid.'

'Nothing at all?'

'No.'

'So you could have been pushed and not been able to remember it. Or do you recall anything about the car that hit you?'

Penny was shaking her head.

'The nurse says you are not too badly hurt, so the car must have been going fairly slowly, yet he sped off without stopping. Why was that, do you think?'

'I don't know, panic, I suppose.'

He pursed his lips in disappointment that

there wasn't more to get his teeth into then shut his note book and put it away in his pocket.

'Well, let us know if you have any more trouble, miss.'

He said it as though there was a strong possibility that there might be and Penny shivered. He wandered away down the ward and Penny closed her eyes . . .

It was nearly noon when a taxi deposited her on the drive in front of the Hall. Stiffly she made her way over the grass to the boathouse. The dogs went hysterical when she entered. Penny shooed them all out then went to make herself a coffee.

On her way out with the dogs later that afternoon, she came to an abrupt halt at the sight of the red sports car parked in the driveway. The very thought of seeing Roger Fenleigh again made her chest tighten and her stomach turn. She tried to convince herself it was because she hated him, but she knew that wasn't true. Was she afraid of him? Maybe, afraid of what he represented, power, money, strength, all the things she had learned to yearn for as a child, while acknowledging the effect the lack of them had over her young life.

She tried to analyse why she felt as she did. He was good to look at, she had to give him that, well over six feet tall with fair hair and brown eyes that were as hard and cold as clay soil on a wet day. Handsome, some might call him, with his straight nose, generous mouth and lean cheeks. What was it that made her tremble whenever they met, if it was none of these things?

He failed to appear and Penny let go of a sigh of relief as she passed beyond the house and turned the corner of the kitchen garden. When the garden door creaked then opened, Penny's nerves could take no more and she cried out as she stumbled to one side. The dogs came running back to her as Roger, eyeing her bandages, growled, 'What the devil have you been doing now?'

Her good hand had risen to protect the damaged elbow.

'I was knocked down in town. The police thought I was pushed, actually,' she said, emphasising the last word, 'but it didn't work because I still won't sell.'

She started to limp off down the path.

'Hold on a minute! What do you mean, you were pushed?'

He had come out on to the path with every intention of following her, Penny realised.

'There was a witness who told the police she saw someone push me.'

Her chin rose, her defiant gaze connecting with his.

'And did someone push you?'

'I couldn't remember.'

'How badly were you hurt?'

His eyes searched every inch of her body as

though he really was concerned, Penny thought, as her insides twisted with pain. His gaze came back to her face and what he saw there made him scowl.

'What did you mean by, it didn't work?' he asked as though his brain had only just caught up with her meaning.

Penny was still in a defiant mood although her legs shook with the effort of holding her there when all she really wanted to do was turn and run.

'I can think of only one person who has any reason to want me out of the way.'

His bellow of rage gave her feet wings as she raced down the path, the pain in her knee numbed by her fear of the reactions of the man behind her. He didn't follow her and once beyond the park wall, she sank down on to the grass. Tears ran down her cheeks to drip off her chin. Why was she allowing him to upset her like this, she asked herself over and over again.

It was soon into a warm May and over the past weeks, Penny had kept herself busy putting Clyde through some fairly intensive training. Now, barring the odd slip up, he was reasonably well behaved. Wandering down the overgrown track that led to the rear entrance of the estate, Penny saw the promise of summer's new foliage.

A scream of brakes tore through the peaceful afternoon. The high-pitched but

short-lived cry of an animal in distress had
Penny running down the lane. With heart
pounding in her ears, she came to a halt in the
broken-down entrance to the drive. Tuck
lumbered behind her, and Bonnie broke from
the cover of the undergrowth to catch up and
pass them.

The flashy red sports car was slewed
sideways across the road. A familiar figure
bent over the black and white dog. Roger's
back was towards her and he knew nothing of
her arrival until Bonnie slipped over the road
and lay down on the verge, head on her paws,
eyes missing nothing. He turned then and saw
Penny standing in the gateway, the old
retriever nuzzling her hand. Sick to her
stomach she made to cross the road, but he
stood up and blocked her path.

'I wouldn't,' he said, placing his hands on
her shoulders.

'Let me pass.'

She saw Clyde's head lift in a helpless
gesture as he recognised her voice. Thrusting
Roger to one side, she moved across the road
and dropped to her knees by the young dog's
side. She spoke quietly to him as she breathed
into his face, her hands sliding over his head.
Tears blinded her.

Later, she was aware of Roger's hands as he
raised her to her feet. He tried to pull her
close but she shrugged him off, so he left her
standing by the car while he took his coat from

the passenger seat and gently wrapped Clyde's body in it and placed him on the back seat.

She watched him as though in a dream, then taking hold of the two dogs by their collars, she crossed the road once more and made her way back up the overgrown lane. At the boathouse, she stopped and stood looking out across the river, sparkling and bubbling over its stony bed. Breathing deeply she thrust balled fists into her jeans pockets.

She was in the rocking chair, tears falling unrestrained down her face, the dogs in silent homage at her knee, when the door opened. Penny knew who had entered and that he was coming towards her. Always suspicious, Bonnie rumbled a deep warning in her throat.

Rubbing her eyes with the back of her hand to clear her sight. Penny said wearily, 'Get out.'

'I suppose it's useless to say how sorry I am,' he said, thrusting his clean handkerchief into her hand. 'I did try to avoid him, you know, but he ran straight at me.'

'Where is he?'

'In the stables. I could take him away.'

'No! Leave him,' she cried. 'I'll see to him myself. He must be buried where no-one will disturb him.'

Despite her determination not to do so, the tears began to flow again.

'God, I would have given anything for this not to have happened,' he said and before either dog knew what he was about, Penny was hauled out of the chair and into his arms. She rested gratefully against the strength of his body while he spoke words of comfort. She curled like a stray kitten into the warmth of his shirt. The weight of his hand was surprisingly light as it stroked her hair and his lips, when they moved from her temple to her mouth, offered all the comfort she could have wished for.

'You must tell me where you want Clyde buried and I will see to it.'

They were now seated on the settee, his arm protectively around her shoulders. Penny moved her head as though trying to see past something that was obscuring her view.

'Now, I'm going to make you that old British standby, a cup of tea,' he said, 'which will give you time to tidy yourself up.'

Bonnie rushed forward as he stood up, and laid her head possessively on Penny's knee. She should be screaming, Penny thought, turning him out of her home. He had knocked Clyde down. She had never hated anyone in her life, never harboured resentment against the circumstances of her past. Why then did this one man have the power to inflict upon her all the evils of Pandora's box?

The cup rattled in its saucer as she took it from his hand.

'I would like you to go now, please. I just want to be by myself.'

Her voice wavered as she kept her eyes averted from his face. He stood in silent contemplation for several nerve-stretching seconds, then left without a word.

Clyde was buried the next day on the hillside above Greensfield Park. Roger had done all the preparation and was there with her. As they turned away to go back down the hill, he turned to her.

'It was you I saw up here the day I fell through the floor. You were standing on this very precipice, like a vision carved from the same stone.'

Their eyes met, hers wounded, his challenging, then she turned and walked off.

A letter came from the Richmond Trust next day, stating that there was a dispute as to the legal ownership of the diaries which may or may not involve them in a legal battle. They were sorry, therefore, that they were no longer interested in the property. A further letter came from Elvera Minhurst to say that her offer would stand for an additional month, after which time she would have to look elsewhere.

Bumping into Simon Osbourne in the village sent warning bells ringing through Penny's head.

'Hello, what brings you out here?' she asked.

'I was on my way to see you actually. I heard about the accident to your dog and wanted to

71

say how sorry I was.'

He looked slightly uncomfortable, Penny thought, and worried that it meant that he was carrying another message from Roger.

'I don't suppose you have time for a drink,' he said.

'You aren't here on business then?' she asked, relieved.

'Oh, no. I had a client in Morpeth and decided to stop off here on my way home.'

'Well, I'd love a drink, thank you.'

They moved on up the street to The Angel Hotel where Simon took her arm to escort her inside. Apart from two elderly men standing at the bar, the lounge was empty. Penny took a seat in the curve of the window while Simon went to buy their drinks.

'Pineapple and tonic, is that right?'

'Yes, thank you.'

He placed beer mats under their glasses and sat down beside her.

'Roger told me you had been hurt in a road accident. Are you all right now?'

'Yes, fine, it wasn't anything too dreadful. A sore arm and knee and a bump on the head.'

'He said you thought someone had pushed you.'

Penny shook her head angrily.

'I said no such thing. I told him the police had a witness who said she saw someone push me. I could remember nothing.'

He smiled apologetically.

'You have had some rotten luck lately.'

Penny watched the bubbles come to the surface of her drink.

'Your friend has put a stop to my hopes of the Trust taking over the estate. Did he tell you that?' she said quietly.

'I heard about it, yes,' Simon replied, frowning.

'I don't know what I am going to do now. I've lodged the house with an estate agent but he said that big houses weren't moving all that well at the moment. Of course, Ms Minhurst is still interested and she is leaving her offer open for another month. Do you know her by any chance?'

'Yes, I do. She and Roger have been seeing each other off and on for the past three years. She's a great professional.'

'What does she do exactly?'

'She's a film producer, documentaries. She travels a lot, like Roger. They have much in common.'

'Why do they want Greensfield Park now their business venture has fallen through? Is property like Greensfield so much in demand by developers that they can find a new building company at the drop of a hat? He still hopes I will sell it to him, doesn't he?'

'I suppose so, though I do think Elvera is pushing him to buy it as a home base. Look, I don't want to talk business. Can I persuade you to have dinner with me one evening?'

He reached forward eagerly and covered her hand with his own.

'I think you could do with a bit of cheering up.'

Penny was taken aback, both by the news that Roger Fenleigh really was interested in buying Greensfield as a home and Simon's sudden offer of an evening out. His open features held no threat of trouble and Penny willingly accepted.

She walked home, picked up the dogs and together they climbed the hill and sat down by Clyde's grave. Already the tough moorland grass and bracken were encroaching. Penny cleared it off and, collecting stones, began to build a cairn over the small patch of earth.

On their return home, there was a note pushed under the door. Thinking it must have been left by Claire, Penny picked it up. There was only a handful of words in large capitals on one sheet of paper. It had a funny little dog on the top of the page and read, ONE DOWN TWO TO GO. A shiver of fear ran through Penny. Who on earth was behind this horrible gesture?

CHAPTER SIX

Her anger and frustration at finding the sinister note with no indication of whom the sender might be sent her straight down to Claire's early the next morning. She showed Claire and the family the anonymous note and was comforted by their belief that it would come to nothing.

'Just some sick fool taking advantage of Clyde's accident to get even.'

Penny searched her mind for any reason why someone other than Roger Fenleigh might want to get even, as Billy had put it. The few people she knew in the village were all on friendly terms with her and to the best of her knowledge she had upset no-one. So she burned the note and put the incident to the back of her mind, as Claire advised. Still, she was careful never to take the dogs near the road again.

Now the warmer weather had arrived Penny did most of her writing and sketching outside, on a fallen tree by the river. Arthur found her sitting there the following afternoon.

'Claire wants you to see this morning's paper,' he said, handing her a copy.

'What's in it? Something about the Hall again?'

He gave a shrug.

'Got to be getting back, work needs doing.'

He ambled off before Penny could ask him what it was that she was supposed to be looking for. She set her sketching material aside and opened up the newspaper. In a local news column on the fourth page a heading stated WEALTHY BUSINESS TYCOON DEPRIVED OF FAMILY SEAT. The article went on to tell how a local landowner had married a young employee who was nursing him abroad when he died. As the deceased's new wife, she had disinherited the last member of an old, well-known local family.

Penny set the paper aside and stared out across the water to where a family of moorhens was making its way swiftly downriver. She hugged herself close and bent over as though in pain. So it was out, the word of her marriage, for all the world to see and snigger about. The cruelty of it was a stabbing ache in her chest. Everywhere she went people would think of her as Roger Fenleigh did, that she had married an old man for his money.

It was a hate that was hurting her—hate for her own vulnerability, hate for Roger Fenleigh and his hard-faced friend, Elvera. It was anger, too, at Charlie, for not being here. It was so terrible, it frightened her. At four o'clock she could contain herself no longer and knew she must see Roger.

Roger had just returned from a business meeting in London when he was greeted by

76

Elvera with the news that Penny Chesterton had been hanging around wanting a word with him.

'What, here at the apartment?' he asked somewhat surprised.

'Everywhere, apparently. I came over after getting back from that Turkish earthquake to find poor Cleaver, the doorman, had been pestered out of his wits by the woman. No sooner had I stepped inside than Simon rang to say he had given her your address. Hopefully she has decided to sell us the estate.'

Roger shrugged out of his jacket and walked across to the drinks cabinet where he poured himself a whisky. Elvera was seated in a large armchair, her feet tucked up beneath her. Her attractiveness was undeniable, but tonight for some reason his desire for her had vanished. He hadn't missed her use of the word us, when she referred to the purchase of the Hall.

'So you didn't get to talk to her?' he asked.

'No,' she replied, shaking her head.

'So where has she gone? Did she leave a message downstairs?'

'Not to my knowledge. I just wish she'd see sense, hand over the Hall and stay out of our way. At least she has one dog less now to pester us. That alone will be a blessing.'

'That was an unfortunate accident, and should I become the owner of the Hall I intend to have a dog of my own, incidentally,' he said, his eyes narrowing.

She laughed up into his face.

'You must do as you wish, of course. You will be lord of the manor, as they say.'

A deep frown darkened his brow.

'That is supposition. If Penny won't sell, there is not much we can do about it.'

'Penny, is it, eh?'

Elvera's nose twitched as though she had a dirty smell beneath it.

'She will sell, wait and see,' she added with a cat-like grin.

'What are you up to, my dear? I recognise a certain display of confidence.'

'I have just completed a good job. I have every right to feel confident.'

'Of course you do and I failed to congratulate you.'

She was smiling again as Roger swallowed down the rest of his drink then reached for his jacket.

'Where are you going? I thought we were having a night in.'

'I'm going over to Greensfield to find out what's going on. It must be urgent if she came all the way over here. I can't phone her. She doesn't have a telephone,' he said as Elvera made to protest.

'What can be so urgent that it can't wait until tomorrow? Oh, well, wait for me and I'll come with you.'

'I don't think that's a good idea. Help

yourself to something to eat and I'll be back shortly.'

She looked extremely put out.

'Why go chasing after her now? I can look after whatever it is she wants tomorrow.'

'Are you jealous, afraid I am going to pursue her for her property?

'Jealous? Of what?'

Roger's mouth lifted at the corners as he saw the honest incredulity in her expression. It really would never occur to her that his interest may have wandered. The realisation rubbed at his pride.

*   *   *

Penny was sitting down to her supper when a loud knock on her door had her jump to attention. The dogs barked as she went to open the door. A large figure blocked the twilight.

'You wanted to see me, I believe.'

Penny stood in the doorway, numb with shock. The hate and anger had not lasted, now there was only a gnawing ache.

'It isn't a convenient time,' she managed to get out in a whisper.

'Why, are you entertaining? No, I thought not.'

Roger eased past her and reached down to quieten the dogs, who immediately fawned all over him.

'I thought we understood one another.'

'So did I but I was wrong.'

'You have to find a buyer for the Hall and I want to buy it.'

'I underestimated how far you would go to own this estate.'

'Now you are talking in riddles,' he said, straightening to his full height. 'Why don't we sit down and you tell me what all the panic is about?'

'I have told you it is not a convenient time and now I must ask you to leave.'

'Well, you can ask but I am not going until I know what brought you to batter on my door.'

'I did not batter on anywhere. I went to your apartment and was told by the porter that you were not in but that Ms Minhurst was available. She sent a message down to say that if I had reconsidered her offer, a letter would be sufficient.'

A nerve twitched along his jaw.

'Well, I'm here now and here I stay until you explain.'

He marched into the room, eyed her small meal of scrambled egg on the table by the rocking chair and sat himself down on the settee.

The anger in her rose easier this time, bubbling up in her throat until she had to clench her teeth to hold it in check.

'Where are you going?'

His head snapped round as she came out of

the kitchen wearing a jacket. He was across the room and holding a hand against the door as she struggled to open it.

'Get out of my way,' she exploded angrily.

'This is stupid! Your supper is getting cold.'

'Either get out of my way or get out of my house.'

He took her by the shoulders and shook her.

'Is it something I'm supposed to have done?'

Unable to hold back the anger any longer it burst out in a torrent.

'People like you make me want to throw up. Presenting one face to the world and doing your dirty deals behind their backs.'

'What the devil are you talking about, you stupid woman?'

'It was you who made the Trust back down when they thought I wasn't the legal owner of the diaries, wasn't it? And it was you who had me knocked down in town. Then you killed my dog and wrote that disgusting note, to frighten me into selling you the Hall, didn't you? Now, deny being responsible for that if you can.'

She broke away from him to thrust the newspaper at his chest.

'What note?' he asked, catching the paper, and glancing swiftly at the column heading. 'You're wrong, you know. I had nothing to do with this or this note you talk about. As for the rest, I think you know the truth. You just don't want to believe it,' he said, holding her with a penetrating stare.

Then he was gone.

Claire and Billy tried to console her next morning when she called in after doing some shopping, but she was frightened. She had lost her temper and now Roger Fenleigh was aware that she blamed him for all the seemingly unrelated incidents that had occurred lately.

'I don't understand, Penny,' Claire said quietly. 'Why would he go to such extreme lengths to get hold of the estate?'

Penny stood up and began to pace the floor.

'I don't pretend to understand his motives. It's just that everything has changed so horribly since he arrived.'

'Has it really, love? OK, so you lost the interest of the Trust people. Are you sure you couldn't get Fenleigh to buy the house, contract and all? It seems to me that would be the perfect solution. You would be richer than you have ever been, you could keep your home, the villagers could continue to fish and walk and play in the woods.'

Penny stared at her friend.

'You think I'm exaggerating it all,' she said wearily.

'A little maybe,' Claire admitted.

On her way home along the woodland path, Penny stopped to listen. The wind that had blown all morning had died and now the air was still. Tuck stood beside her, luxuriating in the time to sniff at every stick and leaf within his reach, while Bonnie raised a family of ducks from their nest. They sped across the water to land by the far bank.

Claire was right, she must try to find and restore the peace within herself. But how on earth was she to convince Roger to sign the contract stipulating no development?

Once home, Penny dressed in a pretty candy-striped shirtwaister dress. Its halter neck and low back exposed her pale golden tan. Heeled, strappy sandals completed the outfit for her evening out with Simon. He arrived just after eight and they drove down to The Apple. It was a warm evening considering the earliness of the year and Penny carried only a wool cardigan with her for later.

'Shall we agree not to mention a certain acquaintance? Then perhaps we can get on and enjoy ourselves,' he said as he led her into the main dining-room.

Penny smiled back.

'Agreed.'

She buried her head in the menu. Once they had selected their choice and handed the menus back to the waiter, Simon asked about her work. She told him of an offer for her new book and of the interest a film company had shown in securing the rights. As an accountant, he was naturally interested in the financial side of the publishing business and happily explained certain aspects of her work that had always been left in the hands of her agent.

They had a very pleasant meal and were laughing at some reminiscence of Penny's as they stood to leave, when Roger and Elvera entered the dining-room. Elvera, dressed all in black with heavy gold jewellery at her neck and wrist, her flaming red hair foaming about her shoulders, came rushing over to their side. Roger followed with seeming reluctance and gave them a narrow-eyed stare before nodding to Simon.

'Why, hello, this is a most convenient meeting,' Elvera gushed. 'We have been up to the Hall actually, in the hope that we could change your mind. I've found the most wonderful interior design people. Of course, there would be a lot of renovation work to do first.'

She continued on in this vein before a completely taken aback Penny.

'I don't think Penny has actually made up her mind to sell yet,' an embarrassed Simon broke in.

Elvera dismissed him with an enquiring look and continued to bombard Penny with her plans for the Hall.

'Just think of the advantage of having neighbours who are only there on high days and holidays. The rest of the time you would have the entire place to yourself. Isn't that what you wanted?'

'There is still the question of the contract,' Penny began.

'Ah, yes, the contract,' Roger said for the first time. 'We could agree to that, I'm sure. There are always legal loopholes for getting out of this type of contract.'

A shocked Simon was about to remonstrate with his friend when a pale Penny turned to him and suggested they should leave.

It was two o'clock in the morning when Bonnie's whining woke her. 'Do you want to go out, sweetheart?'

It wasn't like Bonnie to disturb her during the night, but thinking that the dog might have picked something up and was feeling sick, Penny stumbled from the bed. At the door, the dog growled low in her throat but made no attempt to go out.

'What is it, girl?'

Penny was puzzled at the dog's behaviour. After a while when she still wouldn't budge, Penny brought her back in and closed the door. She had to order Bonnie back to bed. For the rest of the night Penny was kept awake by the dog's restlessness.

Next morning, on returning to the boathouse after walking the dogs, Penny was horrified to find the door standing open and the interior a mess. Drawers had been emptied, their contents flung around the room. Paint was sprayed in spirals down the walls and across the window. Paintings were smashed, the kitchen was a shambles of broken crockery and turned out cupboards. The dog baskets were overturned and their contents ripped. But what really made her cry out was her broken beloved rocking chair.

CHAPTER SEVEN

'Stay back,' she ordered the dogs in case they injured themselves on the broken glass and crockery and, biting her lips to stop them trembling, she pushed forward into the mess and made a gentle attempt to right the rocker. The back spindles were splintered where the burglar had put his boot through it, and one rocker was so badly twisted Penny was doubtful it could ever be repaired.

With tears choking her throat, she looked around for a place to start. How was she ever going to manage? She would need extra cleaning materials to remove the paint. With a sob, she collected the dogs and tramped down to the village and Claire.

'Don't get too comfortable,' Claire warned her as she made to pick up the van keys from the table. 'We're going straight back up. Billy, phone the police and tell them what's happened. Send them up the main drive and I'll watch out for them.' Turning to Penny she said, 'Come on love, let's see what's to do.'

Penny climbed into the front of the van while the dogs were bundled into the back. Bottles of turpentine and disinfectant were piled around Penny's feet as mops, buckets and rags were thrown in the back with the dogs. No-one spoke as a grim-faced Claire drove them back through the village and out to the main drive of the Hall.

When Claire saw the state of the little flat she was nearly in tears. 'Do you still maintain Roger Fenleigh was responsible for this?'

Her voice quivered with anger, but Penny shook her head.

'Not personally, of course not, but who else would go to these lengths? I have nothing of value except the property I live on.'

Claire was nodding her head.

'I must apologise, Pen. I really thought you were exaggerating.'

'He must hate me very much.'

'Rubbish, he's just a greedy devil and I shall tell him so at the first opportunity.'

After agreeing that they mustn't touch anything until the police arrived, they posted themselves by the van and waited. A police car drew up behind the van twenty minutes later and a male and female constable climbed out. Penny told them what had happened and they all walked together to the boathouse. After a quick look around they agreed that the place was in a terrible state. Penny was asked to check on her personal possessions which she did and confirmed that nothing had been stolen.

'Then there is nothing we can do, I'm afraid. It'll be kids. This sort of thing they call a prank these days, and unless you can catch them at it there's not a lot we can do.'

'Kids!' Claire snorted. 'Go on, Pen, tell them who you really think is responsible,' she said, giving her friend a nudge.

'Is there someone you know who may have been responsible?' the woman police officer asked looking directly at Penny.

Penny took a firm grip on herself. He's not going to get away with it, she told herself, not this time.

'Yes.'

'I see, then you had better come down to the station and make a formal complaint.'

'You pop off with them now, Penny, and I'll see to the flat,' Claire said, then she turned to the policeman. 'How will she get home?'

'Is that van yours?'

'Yes.'

'Then it would be better if you both came. That way you can bring her home when she's ready. I wouldn't worry about the flat. I don't think it's going anywhere.'

They climbed back into the van and followed the police car to the nearest town, ten miles away. In a small interview room in the station, Penny told her story to two officers. She started with the accident in town and tried to be as unbiased as possible. They let her talk uninterrupted.

When she had finished, one of the policemen said, 'So the only time you can actually connect Mr Fenleigh to this charge is when he knocked down your dog?'

Penny began to see the enormity of her accusation but was determined to stick to her story seeing no other explanation for the recent happenings.

'I suppose so, yes.'

'And that could have been an accident?'

'Yes.'

'There could be simple explanations for all of these events, wouldn't you say?'

'Yes,' Penny had to agree.

'But you don't think so?'

'No.'

'Well, I'll tell you what we'll do, Mrs Chesterton. We'll put the matter to Mr Fenleigh and see what he has to say.'

He stood up and held out his hand. The interview was over, she was being dismissed. She and Claire left the station and drove in silence back to Greensfield Park.

'Well?' Claire demanded when the silence in the van grew strained. 'What did they say?'

'Nothing much. They took my statement, then said they would be getting in touch with Roger Fenleigh to get his side of it. Oh, Claire, do you really think with his position and money they are going to take any notice of a nobody like me?'

'They'll have to.'

That evening, after working all day on the flat, Penny was staying with Claire as it was going to take a further day before it would be fit for habitation once more. Penny asked if

90

she could phone Simon to let him know what had happened.

'Of course, feel free, but isn't he a friend of Fenleigh's?'

'Yes, he is, but he's my friend, too. At least I hope he is.'

Simon was shocked when he heard the news and agreed to meet her in The Apple Inn on the following evening. After convincing him she was all right and staying with a friend that evening he eventually rang off.

'What was all that about?' Claire expressed curiosity.

'I want to explain to him why I accused Roger and see what his reactions are. I'm hoping he will help me find out who put those articles about me in the paper and who was hired to ransack my home. If what I said to the police is going to be made to stick then I am going to need proof.'

'Good thinking.'

'Only because I'm so mixed up and scared, Claire. Six months ago I wouldn't have dreamed of accusing anyone of anything.'

'I know, love, but that was because you have been sheltered all your life. First, although it wasn't ideal, there was the children's home, making all the choices for you, then there was Charlie. It's a bad world out there, Pen. You have to toughen up if you don't want people tramping over you.'

When she told Simon what she wanted of

him the following evening, he was speechless.

'My dear girl, if Roger was so desperate for the property, and I can't for the life of me think he would be, he's quite capable of picking you up bag and baggage and dumping you on the local tip. No, you have got yourself one angry tiger by the tail when he hears of this. What on earth persuaded you that Roger was responsible?'

Penny was feeling uncomfortable. Had she made a ghastly mistake?

'But who else?' she begged. 'If Clyde's death was an accident and children wrecked my flat, who was it who pushed me into the road in Newcastle? Who was responsible for the articles in the newspaper?'

Simon's face had taken on a more serious expression.

'The articles were news items, just that. Anyone can be a source of information. And your accident in Newcastle, well, maybe it was just an accident. Someone thought you were pushed, but you don't remember being pushed so perhaps you weren't.'

'What do you think he will do when the police tell him what I have said?'

'Probably sue you for defamation of character.'

'What?' she hissed angrily. 'After the things that were printed about me!'

'The inference was wrong but the words were correct in your case. You did marry an old man, you did disinherit Roger. Your accusation of Roger has no substance at all until you can provide some evidence.'

'I was hoping you would help me find that.'

'I wouldn't be much of a friend if I did, now, would I?'

Simon's expression was all sympathy now.

'Let things lie. Don't push things any further and I'll let you know when he simmers down a bit.'

'I hate that man,' Penny burst out with quiet ferocity. 'I know he's your best friend, but I hate him.'

'Well, he can't hate you so much.'

Penny looked up from the beer mat she had been pushing back and forth on the table.

'What do you mean?'

'I've never known him back down over a deal like he has this time.'

He took the mat gently from between her fingers.

'Back down? He hasn't backed down. He is still determined on my selling to him.'

'Roger is rich enough to have walked away from the Trenchard deal. He only looked into it as a way of getting rid of an unwanted property.'

'Then why is he pushing me so hard to sell to him?'

'You tell me or better still ask him. Let me get you another drink.'

He went off to the bar, leaving Penny totally

confused. On one hand she had Roger Fenleigh threatening her into selling him the property and on the other she had Simon telling her that Roger wasn't interested. She shook her head. Simon must be mistaken. The thought came to her suddenly that perhaps it was Elvera who was keen to own the Hall.

Simon returned with fresh drinks and because she was thirsty she drank swiftly.

'Would your friend push the sale for Ms Minhurst?' she asked.

Simon considered this then said, 'Perhaps. I know Elvera is keen on the idea of playing lady of the manor. But if she is hoping Roger will marry her and settle down to a life of domesticity, then she is hoping in vain. He's not the marrying type.'

'Would she purchase for herself?'

'Definitely not. She hasn't the funds and her career always comes first.'

By the end of the evening, not being used to much alcohol, she was feeling decidedly woosy as they left the bar. Simon laughed as he led her out to the carpark. They drove back to the Hall in silence. She tried to say good-night and make a dignified exit of the car but her legs wouldn't do what she wanted them to do! Simon came around to her rescue and with an arm securely around her waist guided her across the lawn to her door.

'I have to walk the dogs,' she whispered in his ear.

'We'll get you inside first,' he said, taking her key from her hand. 'Then I will walk the dogs for you.'

'No,' she protested as he opened the door and switched on the light.

'Good Lord!' she exclaimed.

The flat had been cleaned and tidied but its very bareness lay witness to its terrible assault. The shock had sobered Penny who stood shaking in his arms.

'You had better get tucked in directly while I'm out with the dogs,' he insisted.

Penny climbed out of her clothes, angry with herself for drinking so much. She was curled up in a cold huddle when Simon returned.

'Would you like me to stay over? I can sleep on the settee.'

'No, it's not comfortable now. They broke a spring. But thank you for the offer. Lock up on your way out and put the key under the eaves. Good-night, Simon.'

'Good-night Penny,' he whispered as he bent over to smooth back her hair. 'I can see why Roger stays.'

The next morning Penny wasn't sure if she had heard Simon right the night before. She discounted it and went back to wondering if the police had questioned Roger yet.

She was busy working on a sketch of an otter she had caught on film a few weeks earlier when a large shadow loomed over her, blotting out the light from her drawing pad.

95

Sitting on her favourite fallen log, she twisted round to look up against the sun.

'You make a pretty picture sitting there. How is an unsuspecting stranger to know that the core of the fruit is rotten?'

Penny jumped up, spilling her work across the ground.

'I suppose this is because the police have been to see you.'

Roger Fenleigh was six feet two in his stocking feet with broad shoulders. For a desk man he was extremely fit and Penny's movements faltered as she faced him. Then her chin came out and her eyes sought his. 'I refuse to be threatened.'

'I haven't threatened you, yet. I want to know what happened here on Tuesday morning.'

Penny swallowed.

'I was broken into. Nothing was stolen but several things were destroyed. The place was in a terrible mess, as the police will confirm.'

'They already have. What made you think I would stoop to arranging such a thing?'

His voice was low and icy as Penny watched him like a mesmerised rabbit.

'Who else could have given the newspapers facts about my marriage to Charlie? I overheard you telling Simon what you thought of me then. I've had no reason to think your opinion has changed.'

'Haven't you?'

'No.'

'And do you believe I deliberately ran down your dog?'

She was shaking like a leaf in a breeze and rubbing her arms as though to ward him off when she turned to stare out over the river.

'When I realised how nearly you could have been hurt, I could have killed you myself. Have you any idea what might have happened to you if you had been there when they came?' he was saying.

'The dogs would have gone for them.'

'A rheumatic Labrador and a soft collie? The intruders would have cracked their skulls open and yours, too, when they had finished with you.'

'The police said they were children.'

'Do you believe that?'

'I don't know.'

'No, you don't.'

Something in his voice made her turn her face up to his and what she saw there left her breathless. Was it concern, she asked herself afterwards, or something more? Her heart bumped in her chest as she watched Bonnie follow him back to his car.

*   *   *

Elvera had only that morning finalised a profitable deal for film coverage of an exclusive interview in Latin America when

Roger walked into her office. She began to tell him about it but tailed off as she noticed his lack of interest.

'What do you expect to gain if I buy Greensfield Park?' Roger asked.

She sat back and gave him a hard look.

'I would enjoy being your hostess.'

'You wouldn't be harbouring ideas of marriage, would you, Elvera? I didn't think either of us thought like that.'

She gave a sharp laugh.

'Don't worry, that's no more appealing to me than it is to you.'

'Just hostess, eh?'

He made no attempt to sit down.

'What is this?'

She leaned back in her swivel chair swinging it back and forth. The red hair was tied back with a tortoiseshell clip. Brown linen slacks and an amber top set off the elongated eyes that shone with mockery.

'I don't think we are sliding along quite as we used to,' he said. 'Something jars and you know how I dislike rough edges.'

'Then tell me what it is and I'll see if I can smooth it out for you.'

She rose from the chair and came towards him wrapping her arm through his. He frowned down at her.

'The boathouse was vandalised three days ago. Penny's got it into her head that I was somehow to blame.'

'Why would the stupid girl think that? It's obviously not a safe place to live anyway with all and sundry wandering around in those woods.'

'I agree with you but there is also the matter of a newspaper article whose information she says no-one but herself, her lawyer and I knew about, and an accident in town when she says she was pushed off the pavement in front of a car.'

'Paranoia, definitely,' Elvera said over her shoulder as she made her way back to her desk and sat down. 'If she is as concerned as all that about the articles and accidents why doesn't she just accept your offer and find somewhere else to live?'

'Why don't you pay her a visit?' Roger said. 'Tell her you've upped your price to match mine and that you are prepared to sign her contract and see what she says.'

Elvera raised an eyebrow.

'You think it might work?'

'It might. It's worth a try.'

'Right,' she said with a grin.

Roger was puzzled. Why was Elvera so keen on pushing this matter of the Hall? Was she really satisfied with their relationship as it was? It had suited him well in the past to have her nearby, but if she was growing tired of the situation he would have to quosh it. He wasn't the marrying type and even if he was . . .

He closed his eyes and saw again the flash

of a red anorak on a hillside. His lids opened slowly and he stared at Elvera across the office. Was she really as impervious to jealousy as she implied?

CHAPTER EIGHT

Claire was helping to decorate the boathouse. The well-washed graffiti was now mere shadows of pink and easily covered by a fresh coat of cream paint. Billy was looking after the shop and Arthur had promised to keep an eye on him.

'The police must have spoken to Fenleigh by now and yet you say there has been no response from him?' Claire queried.

'I didn't say there'd been no response. I simply said he hadn't made a fuss.'

Penny wobbled on top of the ladders, then came down and plonked her tin of paint on to the paper-covered small table and sat down on the edge of the new mattress. Claire took both pots into the kitchen and returned with two glasses of juice.

'So tell me about it.'

'Tell you what?' Penny asked.

'You have seen him since the police talked to him, right?'

'Yes.'

'So what happened?'

Penny sighed.

'He was angry, of course, but he, well, he seemed concerned about my safety.'

'Does that mean he is no longer the villain?'

'I don't honestly know, Claire. Perhaps I'm

becoming paranoid. I just feel so confused.'

'Of course, if you'd met him on the street and he'd asked you out things might have been very different.'

Penny gave her a twisted smile.

'Aren't you forgetting someone?'

'Oh, she can't hold a candle to you.'

'Come on, let's get this painting finished or you will have the villain turning into the handsome prince.'

'Well, isn't he?' Claire demanded, going back into the kitchen to collect the paint.

The next thing Penny heard was a high-pitched scream followed by an almighty crash. She rushed into the kitchen to find Claire flat on her back, filling most of the kitchen floor, while Bonnie sat with a look of surprise on her face, her coat dripping with cream paint.

'Oh, my goodness, Claire, are you hurt? Can you get up?'

Claire struggled to her feet as Penny rescued the paint tins and dropped them into the bin.

'Good grief,' Claire cried as she got to her feet and spied the now cream Bonnie.

Penny ran back into the main room and snatched some plastic sheeting that Claire had brought for the floor. Back in the kitchen she managed to bundle the reluctant collie into the plastic and out on to the veranda. Claire followed her out with a bucket of water and some clothes.

102

'What in heaven's name are we going to do with her?'

'Try and remove some of this paint but first, if you are feeling all right, please mop up the kitchen floor,' Penny suggested as she removed the excess paint from the dog with a pile of paper towels.

Claire had disappeared into the kitchen when a deep mocking voice said, 'Don't you have enough to do inside without painting that poor animal as well?'

The dog's tail swished harder and the black T-shirt and grey jeans the visitor wore were spotted with the same cream rash as the surrounding veranda!

'Oh, dear, I'm so sorry but it's your own fault for coming here in the first place.'

She was struggling to hold on to the dog and slosh her with warm soapy water at the same time.

'Here, let me help you. If I hold her still you can scrub her more easily.'

Penny's jaw fell open momentarily but then she allowed Roger to hold the messy dog, not caring of the damage to his clothes. Their eyes met and a shared smile crossed the divide.

Claire replaced dirty water with clean until at last the dog, soaked through and miserable, looked more her normal self. Penny stood up, stretching her back, and Roger continued to rub the wretched dog dry.

'She should be all right now if she lies out in

the sun,' he said.

They cleared away the refuse and Claire offered them more drinks. Roger accepted the drink, commented on their work in the main room, then made his excuses and left.

'Well, it seems our villain can be quite pleasant when he puts his mind to it,' Claire commented.

Her remark brought the sting of a blush to Penny's cheeks and she wished just for a moment that she was on her own. For what—to savour the smile they had shared? Her conscience kicked in and she offered to treat Claire to a meal at The Angel after all the help her friend had been.

Claire wouldn't hear of it but promised they would celebrate once Arthur had finished repairing the rocking chair and re-varnishing a second-hand set of drawers that Billy had found in a farm sale.

'I don't know what I would have done without you all,' Penny remarked.

'Rubbish, that's what friends are for. Are you saying you wouldn't have done the same for me?'

'Of course I would.'

'There you are then. Now I must be off. Don't go painting any more dogs, will you?'

The flat was as finished as it would ever be, Penny thought several days later, having returned from walking the dogs. The cream walls were hung with some of her own beautiful water colours, the window, clean once more, shone out across the river. The new mattress was made up with pretty new bedding, the old mattress having been burned. The rocking chair was back in its old familiar place, as good as new. Arthur had re-upholstered her settee and all together Penny was well pleased with the results.

*   *   *

Elvera Minhurst, in buttercup yellow overalls with a green scarf tied around her hair, sat on the sun-warmed stone wall of the terrace outside the library window when Penny looked up from some research work she had been doing that afternoon.

'Hello,' she said, rising from her chair and crossing to the open window.

Elvera smiled back and stretched like a sun-warmed cat.

'I came over to see you but when I saw you were working I thought it best not to disturb you. It being such wonderful weather for so early in the year I decided to make the most of it. I'm off to Canada the day after tomorrow.'

Penny stepped aside to allow her to enter the library.

'What did you want to see me about?'

'The house, of course. What else? I've decided to up the offer to match Roger's and I will agree to sign any papers you like about the property's future.'

She side-stepped allowing Penny to pass in front of her.

'That's very generous of you. Can I ask if you intend to live here alone?'

'I don't see that's any of your business.'

'I must appear rude. I don't mean to be but you see I can't help feeling that Roger Fenleigh is behind this offer of yours.'

Elvera shrugged.

'What if he is? I've told you we will sign your contract forbidding any development. We mean it, you know. We have no intention of selling it on. We want to live here. What possible objection can you have to that?'

'I don't believe you. You have already made it clear that you believe there are loopholes in my contract.'

Slim eyebrows rose to elongate the already long face.

'Are you going to sell me this property or not?'

'I don't think you can afford to, Ms Minhurst.'

Penny watched the woman's nostrils flare in anger.

'You'll regret this decision. We are not the kind of people who tolerate being made fools of.'

Penny didn't know what had prompted her to speak as she had. She couldn't bear the thought of Roger and that woman living so close, having them as neighbours, no matter how desperate she was to sell the house. Her face warmed at the thought that she might be jealous. Her teeth bit down on her lip as she watched Elvera climb into her car and disappear down the drive.

Since the incident with the spilled paint, Bonnie, despite all the brushing since her mishap, still looked rather forlorn. Her reactions were slower than normal and Penny was worried about her. In the end she decided to take her to the vet. It meant getting a bus into the market town of Alnwick, ten miles away.

'Nothing wrong with her that I can see,' the vet said on examining the dog. 'Leave her with me for a couple of days and we'll do some tests.'

He lifted the dog down from the table and a nurse arrived to take her off to the boarding kennels.

'Ring me at the end of the week and I'll let you know how we are doing.'

All the way home, Penny worried about what could possibly be wrong with Bonnie. When she rang the vet on Saturday morning, he asked her if she was the only owner.

'Yes.'

'You mentioned the loss of a puppy some weeks ago but that wasn't her puppy, was it?'

'No.'

'And an incident with a pot of paint. There

107

is no question of divided loyalty anywhere, is there?'

'No, none at all.'

'Well, ring me again on Monday. I'd like to observe her more.'

There had been no further contact with either Elvera Minhurst or Roger Fenleigh and Penny was happy to let things drop there. On Monday morning when Penny rang the vet he said she could come in and collect the dog.

'But I would like to talk to you before you leave,' he added.

It was raining hard as she headed across the lawns to the main drive. She spotted Roger's red sports car in front of the Hall. As she turned to head down the drive, he came out of the entrance and she heard the car door shut, then the engine start up. The car drew up alongside her.

'Where are you off to?' he asked through the lowered window.

'I have to go into Alnwick. Bonnie's at the vets. I'm going in to collect her.'

'Let me give you a lift then,' he said in surprisingly friendly tones.

Penny eyed him warily, surprised to find he held no grudge after her confrontation with Elvera Minhurst.

'It must be out of your way,' she said, continuing to walk on.

'Not at all and it will save you getting wet.'

Penny considered waiting at the bus stop

and dodging splashing traffic and decided she would be glad of a lift.

'Thank you.'

She moved around to the other side of the car and got in.

'What's wrong with Bonnie?' he asked as he pushed the car into gear and moved off along the drive and out on to the road.

'They don't know. She began to flag after that episode with the paint, went off her food, lay around all the time, not like herself at all. It's a mystery.'

'She seemed fine when she was over at the Hall the other day.'

'You were at the Hall?'

'I came down to see you after you sent Elvera away with a flea in her ear.'

He turned to look at her and caught the expression on her face. His whole demeanour stiffened as he exploded, 'Not again. What are you suggesting this time, that I have deliberately poisoned your dog?'

Penny shook her head.

'No, of course not.'

But the suspicion lay coiled, ready to leap. Why would Bonnie have gone to the Hall? She had never shown any inclination before to stray. What was it that had attracted her there?

'The vet was very definite that he could find no physical reason for her condition.'

His mouth was pulled taut as he said, 'Well,

whatever the vet said, I am coming with you. If someone has hurt the animal I will want to know who.'

Penny opened her mouth to object but after glancing sideways at his profile decided it might be wiser to give way this time.

The vet was surprised to see her accompanied by such a determined looking character.

'We are achieving nothing keeping her here. All the tests have come back clear. You can take her home with you. I'll give you some medication which is a simple tonic. Give it to her twice a day and we will see how she goes on. My personal opinion is that she is pining, for what, you must have a better idea than I do. My advice to you is to try and find out what it is she is pining for.'

'Surely there must be something you can do,' Roger asked.

'I wish we could,' the vet replied.

Penny heard the tapping of paws coming along the tiled floor of the corridor outside the room. Then the nurse opened the door and let Bonnie in. A miraculous change came over the dog as she hurled herself at an astonished Roger. Such was the force of her enthusiasm that he had to step back to accommodate her whirling body.

'I think we have your answer,' the vet exclaimed.

Now the collie broke away and fawned at

110

Penny's feet.

'You crazy animal, what is the matter with you?' Penny reprimanded the collie.

'You say you took her from a shelter?'

The vet was leaning over, patting the dog.

'Yes,' Penny replied.

'Then the chances are that her previous owner was a man. She hasn't forgotten this and I presume this gentleman lives nearby. She has switched her allegiance, if you like, to him. While basically all dogs are loyal this has caused her some amount of confusion. In other words, she is torn between the two of you and I would suggest you get together and sort this out.'

Roger gave Penny a bewildered shrug as she stared at him with a frown.

'Now what do we do?' she demanded in an angry voice once they were out of the surgery.

He strode across to the car and, unlocking the door, shooed the dog inside.

'Come on, woman, the first thing to do is get home.'

She followed him through the rain and climbed into the passenger seat, smacking the dog on the nose when she would have pushed between the two front seats.

'Don't take it out on the dog. It's not her fault,' he snapped.

'I'm not, but she's not used to travelling in cars. She might have got in your way.'

The old antagonism flared again spoiling

111

what might have been the beginning of an easier relationship. Penny sighed.

'I would be grateful for any suggestions as to how we might solve this problem.'

They turned out of the surgery yard and headed back through the town. He gave her a quick glance through dark, perceptive eyes.

'I could always take her off your hands.'

'No,' she cried.

'Or you could agree to sell me the Hall. As your neighbour she could have free access to me whenever she wanted. She wouldn't even have to cross a road.'

His hands moved smoothly as he changed gear for the climb out of the town and on to the moor road—nice hands, long and slim with clean square-cut nails not pampered and manicured like so many businessmen's hands were. She imagined what it must be like to be held close by such hands, how they might feel on her skin, then she caught herself dreaming. What on earth was the matter with her?

'To be a neighbour, you would have to live there full time.'

'With time off for good behaviour?'

A grim smile twisted his mouth.

What would it be like seeing him most days, knowing he was just across the lawn? Could she bear to watch him with Elvera, seeing the house lit up for parties, watching the comings and goings from the sidelines? Was that what it was all about, she asked herself. Was she jealous of his lifestyle?

Penny turned her head sideways to look at him. But his profile showed no hint of amusement.

'I'll think about it,' she said.

In no time at all they were approaching Greensfield Park. Bonnie sat up and started to whine. Then they became aware of the urgent clanging from a fire engine as it came up behind them. Roger pulled it over to let it pass.

'Some poor devil in trouble.'

'Roger, look!' Penny shouted, reaching across him and nearly forcing him into the ditch.

'What the devil?'

'Oh, no, it's the Hall.'

Now he, too, had seen the spiral of smoke that rose from behind the trees. With a spurt of speed that frightened her he hurled the car in through the gates and up the drive. The tyres screamed to a halt inches from the back of the fire engine that was parked not in front of the Hall but to one side of the drive.

Firemen were running out hose pipes across the lawn to where the boathouse was well alight. There was a sudden flash and bang as a gas cylinder exploded. Penny screamed, tearing herself out of the car and running towards the fire. She ignored Roger's cry and the firemen's warnings as she pelted across the grass. Tuck was in there and she must get to him.

Fear fed adrenaline to her straining heart. She was close enough now to hear the cracks and bangs as the burning wood gave way. She coughed and sneezed as the acrid smoke choked her lungs. The fierce heat scorched her face and she threw up an arm to protect herself. Then she was running no more for two strong arms had wound themselves around her and before she could cry out she was toppled to the ground.

Her chest heaved painfully and her head, when she tried to move it, was jerked back by the hair in a vicious tug. The last thing she heard was the hiss of the hosepipes as blackness claimed her.

CHAPTER NINE

As she climbed up through the fog in her head and the feeling of nausea in her stomach, Penny struggled to reassert her intention.

'Don't be a fool woman,' an angry voice growled in her ear. 'Look over there.'

A long arm came out from behind her and pointed towards the river where a dripping dog was being hauled up on to the bank.

'Tuck, oh, Tuck!'

A wavery voice she barely recognised as her own came from her throat and was followed by a quick intake of breath as she was hauled to her feet and swept up into the arms of Roger Fenleigh.

Some hours later, when everyone but Roger had gone, Penny began to assert herself.

'You can't stay here,' Roger protested for the umpteenth time that day.

'Why not? Nothing has changed in my old room. I'll light a fire, air the bedding.'

'It's a wreck,' he argued. 'Anything could happen to you in this mausoleum and no-one would know. Don't you have a friend in the village? What was her name, Claire, wasn't it? Why can't you stay with her?'

He was following her around the drawing-room of the Hall as she removed dust sheets that billowed dust and made her cough.

'For how long? I've lost my home and everything in it. I'm extremely lucky to have this place to fall back on. I dread to think what would have happened had I not.'

'Let me take you down to The Angel then.'

'I can't afford to live there, even for a short while. Anyway, I rather think they will be full up. It is a busy time of year for them.'

Penny twisted the sheet in her hands. She was frightened, she admitted to herself. But she must find out who was behind all the things that had been happening to her. Was there any doubt now that someone was out to harm her? Surely the police would take notice this time.

As though reading her mind, Roger growled, 'I hope I'm not to be accused of arson on top of everything else.'

He straightened from the mantelpiece, his movements impatient. Tension grew until at last Penny sagged under the weight of it.

'What else am I to think?' she cried. 'Who else even knows I'm alive let alone cares enough to want to kill me?'

'Now you're being hysterical. I'm sure no-one is out to kill you. Frighten you perhaps, but kill you, no, that is quite unthinkable.'

'How can you be so certain unless it's you who wants me out of the way?' A sob caught in her breath as she continued. 'You win, I accept your offer. You can have the Hall and the pasture, but I will retain the woods and build another boathouse. You can hate it as much as you like but you won't get rid of me.'

'You stupid woman! I only wish I did hate you.'

Snatching her into his arms he pressed a firm kiss on to her surprised mouth. Penny's mouth quivered under his and her resistance trembled like a house of cards. The kiss intensified and Penny knew she never wanted it to end. But it did. Their lips parted and Roger stood back as their eyes met. Penny felt that if he let go of her shoulders she would fall in a heap at his feet.

At that moment Tuck lumbered into the room followed by Simon, looking decidedly harassed.

'Sorry to butt in and all that but I arrived the same time as the chief fireman looking for a word with you.'

He turned, addressing himself to Penny.

'This is dreadful, Penny. Anything I can do to help, just say the word.'

'Thank you, Simon.'

Penny smiled gratefully, as the fireman appeared and introduced himself.

'Chief Officer Sanderson, and you must be Miss Chapman, the owner of the property we've just lost. I'm sorry, miss, but I'm afraid it's completely gutted. The fire investigator will be along shortly. I believe you had just finished decorating. Is there any chance there might have been combustible material lying around?'

Penny ran a hand across her eyes.

'Of course not, officer. This wasn't an accident.'

'Well, miss, we will have to see what the investigator makes of it. But for the time being there is very little of your belongings left, I'm afraid.'

Roger's hard voice interrupted.

'Thank you, officer, we'll wait to hear from the investigation.'

Penny turned on him the moment the fire chief had left the room.

'Why did you dismiss him like that? It is my home that has been burned and me he came to speak to. Our conversation had nothing to do with you at all.'

'It does if I'm to be accused of arson before we even know that it was arson. You can't go around slandering people, you know, or you will find yourself in court.'

Penny was at a loss to understand the rapid change in his mood.

'I haven't accused anyone.'

'You were about to.'

'No, I wasn't.'

'Oh, yes, you were. I've been around you long enough now to know I'm not safe from the blame of anything that happens to you.'

'You are a complete rogue, do you know that? Charlie would never have wanted to see you here. I wish I had left you to rot in that bedroom.'

Then, her courage failing fast, she turned and rushed from the room.

The boathouse, as they had said, was gutted. All that remained of her home were a few charred timbers pointing forlornly at the sky and an area of black and broken debris. As she moved down to the river she felt a cold nose push into her hand and, looking down, found Bonnie close by her side. The last fire engine roared off down the drive and curious villagers wandered away down the woodland track back to their homes.

At last all was quiet and Penny sat down on her log by the riverside and let the tears tumble down her cheeks. She felt rather than heard Roger's approach. She knew he was there, standing behind her, waiting for her grief to ease. Perhaps it was the reflection of the lowering sun on the river that warmed the colour of his eyes as Penny rose and turned towards him.

He nodded solemnly.

'There have been mistakes and wrongs on both sides and I would like us to try and sort them out. Will you invite me back to the house?'

Penny felt tension return across her shoulders and around her heart, but he was right. If the truth were ever to be found then it must start with them.

They walked back to the house in silence,

the two dogs following close to heel. Back in the drawing-room, they sat on either side of the empty hearth. He indicated that she should start first. She began by telling him of being abandoned as a baby and never knowing her parents; of growing up in an orphanage and being sent to work as a housemaid when she was sixteen, to Greensfield Park. As she talked, her mind drifted back to that happy time and she was aware of smiling at the memories.

Charlie Chesterton had been a wildly exciting young man in his day, but he was already old when Penny first met him and, it was said, eccentric to the point of madness. She had been at the Hall several weeks when she was caught red-handed by her employer taking a book from the library. It was her first contact with Charlie and one she would never forget.

A sad smile curved her mouth as she remembered the terror that had initially washed over her at the time. Charlie, surprised and delighted to find someone so keen to follow his own love of books, had laughed at her fear and told her that his house was her home. In the following years he had encouraged her curiosity, fostered her thirst for knowledge and widened her views with a madcap description of people and life that made listening to him an adventure in itself.

He was a funny cynic of a man with

twinkling eyes and a mop of grey hair. He became the parent she'd never had and a lifetime's frozen love had melted in the warmth of his constant approval of everything she tried to do.

'I could never have allowed your plans for the estate and I had nowhere else to go. I was prepared to go to any lengths to stop you.'

'And now?'

Her eyes, which had remained downcast all the time she was talking, slid up to his face to gauge his reaction to her story. His eyes were guarded.

'Now I will sell because I have to. I can't afford to live here and your money will allow me to rebuild my home,' she said softly.

Penny watched him stretch out his legs, saw the slow smile tilt the corners of his mouth and ease the lines down the sides of his nose. Her heartbeat quickened. Was what she felt for this man love? She'd been ready to believe evil things of him. Why should she trust him now? Because he'd kissed her a couple of times? Because her heart did silly things when he was around? He wasn't comfortable or fun to be with, like Charlie. There was nothing tender about him, she felt.

'I won't sell it, because I want to live here,' he said.

'And you go with the place, like the musty old furnishing, far more than I would,' came a bitter-sounding voice.

121

Neither of them had heard Elvera enter the house.

'I'm on my way to Canada, on another commission. I have no intention of hiding myself away in this backwater. So, on my return, I doubt we will have reason to see each other again, Roger.'

Penny was startled but Roger had got to his feet and was hustling Elvera from the room.

'That's very wise of you, my dear,' he said, as he ushered her into the hallway and closed the door.

Penny heard voices raised in anger then the bang of a door and a short while later the angry revving of an engine and spraying gravel.

*   *   *

'Has world war three started?' Simon asked watching his friend pace back and forward across his office.

He thought of all the things that had happened since Penny Chapman had entered their lives and changed them for ever. It had been love at first sight for him but he'd realised very early that there was no way it would ever be returned so he had said nothing and knew now he never would. The telephone rang, breaking into his thoughts. He picked it up then held it out to Roger, who crossed the room quickly in one stride.

'Fenleigh here.'

There was a long pause with monosyllabic answers then Roger turned to Simon and gave him a nod. After replacing the receiver he said quietly, 'They've arrested Elvera.'

'Reporting your suspicions to the police was the right thing to do, you know. What made you suspect her in the first place?'

'Her changed attitude. She was pushing for my purchase of Greensfield Hall. She claimed it was for my benefit yet she has never to my knowledge bothered about anyone's comfort but her own. I was so concerned that she was changing her views on marriage, that I missed the obvious. Apparently, for some time now, she has been setting up this new television programme set in a stately home, which would provide a background for the ultimate relaxed intimate interviews of famous people.'

'Greensfield Park!' Simon exclaimed.

'Exactly. I just wish it hadn't come to this. Not that our relationship would have continued. It's been easing off for some time now.'

'Have you heard anything from Penny?' Simon asked.

'No, nothing. It's all very confusing. I've been in the Hall a month now and there is still no sign of Penny or any development by the riverside. It's beginning to look as though she's just taken the money and disappeared.'

'That's not Penny's way. She'll be back and when she is do you intend to tell her it was

Elvera who gave that information to the papers, wrote those letters and had her home vandalised and destroyed?'

'Yes,' he said straightening up, 'if I ever get the chance.'

'I think you're right, but tell me, did Elvera really mean to kill Penny?'

'No, I'm sure she didn't. They were scare tactics that got out of hand.'

On his way back to the Hall, Roger stopped off at a local vet he'd been in touch with. He climbed out of the car and made his way to the kennel compound. His once bright shoes were soon covered with tiny paw prints. One of a litter of collie pups was audacious enough to grab a lace and heave and worry at it until the foot moved, at which point the pup plopped down on his bottom and complained.

'Have you decided which one yet?' the vet asked as he joined Roger. 'A tip is to stand still and wait for one of them to come to you. It always works. There, that little chap is yours,' he said, pointing to the puppy that once more was hanging on to his shoe lace.

'I see what you mean,' Roger said, bending down to pick up the puppy.

Two dark button eyes explored his face then the bundle of fur settled down to chewing his thumb joint. The puppy was black and white with tan markings and what the vet assured him would be a white plumy tail. He was the nearest thing to Clyde Roger could find.

*　　*　　*

Penny walked slowly up to Greensfield Hall, the dogs at her feet, her heart in a turmoil of emotions. Once Roger's cheque was in the bank she had lost no time in booking the dogs into kennels and herself a long holiday. Not sure of her feelings, she had delayed the rebuilding of the boathouse until her return. Having no financial worries now, she had booked into The Angel on her return and would stay there as long as was necessary. A strong talk from Claire the previous evening had left her with a painful night of soul searching. Now, she admitted, stepping out more briskly, she was on her way to set the record straight and offer Roger an abject apology for all the accusations she had hurled against him in the past.

She still felt that someone was out to harm her but she had come to accept that whoever it was behind these threats it was not the man who had stolen Bonnie's love. Biting down on her lower lip she asked herself if she was being completely truthful. Was it only Bonnie who had lost her heart?

There were no builder's vans standing in the drive this morning. It was Sunday. And no sign of the four-wheel drive Elvera used. Was his relationship with the cool Ms Minhurst really over, Penny wondered. He was standing just inside the main entrance when she looked up. She could feel the colour creep up her face as she took in the dark green jeans and paler green sports shirt with its open neck. A knot in her throat made her feel that she was about to choke. He looked as though he was expecting her.

'I hoped you would come. Arthur said you were back,' he said when she faced him on the threshold.

'Arthur?'

'He's been doing some restoration work for me.'

She followed him across the marble hallway, through the green baize door and down the inner hallway to the kitchen. Here the modernisation took her breath away.

'What do you think?'

The room, while being updated, had lost none of its old-world warmth and charm. A multi-coloured mat still lay before the new stove, a padded rocking chair to one side. The welsh dresser and scrubbed wood Victorian table were still there to fit in with the wood front units and work tops.

'It's beautiful. Not what I had expected at all.'

He was watching her face closely as he extended a mug of coffee towards her. They sat down at the table and her hand unknowingly stretched across the surface of memories.

'You love this house, don't you?' he asked.

She nodded.

'Could you live here if it meant taking me with it?'

Penny took a sip of her coffee, surprising herself when she noticed that her hand was steady.

'I came here to apologise, for even thinking that you might be the person responsible, that you might hate me enough to—well, I know now that the accidents and letters could never have been down to you.'

His mouth had turned up at the corners and his eyes had darkened to the colour of warm treacle.

'Would you like to see the rest of the house?'

She couldn't hide the pleasure that lit up inside her.

'Yes, please.'

They finished their coffee, shut the dogs in the kitchen and made their way to the front of the house. A lot of the renovations had been remedial repair work, replacing parts of the oak panelling in the dining-room, repairing damaged plaster work, extensive re-plumbing and rewiring. The library was exactly as it had been for most of its life and the warm feeling it gave to Penny to find it virtually untouched surrounded her in a glow.

The morning-room had been turned into an ultra-modern office with every conceivable technological device.

'This is where I will do most of my work. The library I think of as private and relaxing, the drawing-room and dining-room for entertainment and I eat in the kitchen. Shall we venture upstairs now? I assure you it is quite safe these days. And I won't pretend not to be interested in your opinion of the new bathrooms.'

Penny felt tension melt away and a smile came readily to her lips. She admired each of the bedrooms with their new en suites. When they came at last to the room that had been hers she could only gasp in wonder. The new light wood furniture and soft turquoise furnishings with a dark gold carpet turned what had been a dark double room into a wonderful expanse of light and airy space. The bathroom was sheer pleasure.

'It's like something out of Hollywood,' she whispered.

'Oh, dear, I was aiming for something a little less trashy.'

'I'm sorry, I didn't mean . . . it's, well, wonderful.'

The bath was an enormous sunken Jacuzzi. A large corner shower had replaced the old washstand, with sitting area and glass partition separating a double vanity unit from toilet and bidet. Open glass shelves were piled with turquoise towels, bottles and bowls. The room was aglow with turquoise tiles, gold taps and engraved glass. She turned to him with a wide smile and mischievous twinkle in her eyes.

'Aren't you afraid of getting lost in here all by yourself?'

'At the moment, perhaps, but I'm hoping to rectify that.'

He was standing directly behind her and as a blush warmed her face she ducked her head and brushed past him.

'You didn't answer my question,' he reminded her as they came to a halt at the foot of the main staircase.

'What question was that?'

'In the kitchen I asked you if you could see yourself living here with me?'

'I think Ms Minhurst might have something to say about that, don't you?'

'Not any more,' he said, and Penny's mouth was suddenly dry.

'Come back to the kitchen. There is someone I want you to meet.'

Puzzled, Penny allowed herself to be led away. The kitchen was empty and she swung round, a frown of concern on her face. Roger was lifting something from a box in the corner.

'This little chap is looking for a home,' he said, and placed the sleepy puppy into her arms.

The puppy made a half-hearted attempt to familiarise himself with this new person but found it all too much and fell asleep. Tears glittered in Penny's eyes as she gazed up at

Roger.

'Shall we put him back to bed and perhaps later introduce him to the others?'

Penny handed him over and watched Roger place him in the box. They moved through into the drawing-room with its new wine velvet chairs. Roger held out his hand and pulled Penny into his arms.

'You need have no more fear of accidents or nasty letters. It was all Elvera's doing.'

She stared questioningly up into his face.

'She had ambitious plans of her own for which she needed a large, country home. I think perhaps her plans ran away with her when it came to the vandalism and the fire. The two men in her employ have been arrested and Elvera taken in for questioning. They are out of our lives now.'

Lifting up her face to his he kissed her warmly. The feel of his lips sent her heart soaring, her body relaxed against his and her hands crept up around his neck. The pressure and intimacy of the kiss increased and Penny at last admitted her love for him. Why else was this warmth inside her growing until she felt as though she must die?

'You still haven't answered my question,' he challenged.

'I would love to live here,' she replied, 'with you.'

The relief on his face was evident as he swung her up into his arms.

130

'Now, I can tell you that I love you, Great Aunt Chesterton! I have loved you since the moment I saw you on a dark and gloomy hillside, your red anorak a challenge to life itself. My subsequent accident should have warned me you would be the cause of great upheaval in my life but it will all be worth it if you promise to be my wife.'

'I love you, Roger Fenleigh, and I will indeed marry you,' she said. 'I warn you now, though, that I will impose an influence on all things environmental.'

'And I will listen to you, I promise.'